ABOVE EMPYREAN

ABOVE EMPYREAN

A Novel of the Final Days of the War Against Islamist Terrorism

Bruce Herschensohn

Beaufort Books
New York

First Edition

Library of Congress Cataloging-in-Publication Data
Herschensohn, Bruce, 1932-
Above Empyrean : a novel of the final days of the war on Islamic terrorism / Bruce Herschensohn.
p. cm.
ISBN 978-0-8253-0516-0 (alk. paper)
1. Presidents--United States--Staff--Fiction. 2. Terrorism--United States--Fiction. 3. Jihad--Fiction. I. Title.

PS3608.E777A63 2008
813'.6--dc22

2008015698

Published in the United States by Beaufort Books
www.beaufortbooks.com

Distributed by Midpoint Trade Books
www.midpointtrade.com

Interior design by Maria E. Torres, Neuwirth & Associates, Inc.

10 9 8 7 6 5 4 3 2 1

Printed in the United States of America

Contents

ABOVE EMPYREAN

Preface

THIS STORY IS a fictional projection of what could well be ahead if the United States loses the Global War against Islamist Terrorism. Many Americans today will only accept military engagements, if any, that are brief with few U.S. casualties; somewhat like Grenada or the liberation of Kuwait or the military incursions into Panama or Haiti or Bosnia or Kosovo. Those U.S. efforts were carried out for our interests but they were not fought for the survival of our own nation; they were largely fought for the survival of others. We are now engaged in a war for the survival of the United States and the survival of civilization as we know it.

Shortly after 9-11 our leaders gave advice to the people of the nation to live life as before: to work as we have always worked; travel as we have always traveled; go on vacation when time permits; purchase what we would have purchased before. In summary, other than being vigilant, Americans were told not to change our lives from the normal routine known before 9-11. It was bad advice. Too many willingly adopted that advice and lived with the false perception that the war was no more than a background rather than the foreground of their lives, and the war was little more than an infrequent and unwelcome intrusion on the things they chose to do.

The war did not dominate our time as World War II dominated the time of all Americans in that unified quest for victory. Then, three decades after that victory of World War II came the defeats of Cambodia and South Vietnam. At this writing, losing the *current* war is likely because now our culture has contempt for memory. In an epidemic of amnesia, America has forgotten how we achieved victory in one war and defeat in another.

Although this book is fictional, most descriptions of the U.S. takeover are based on real non-fictional recent takeovers of other nations and territories by tyrannical forces. This story of what could lie ahead was painful to imagine and even more painful to write. But the greatest pain of all will come not if it is written or read, but if it is lived.

CHAPTER

1

The Revolution Suceeds

ELI JARED HAD gray hair, gray suits, and gray dreams. The green of life had disappeared.

At least Eli Jared had known decades of deep green and those decades acted as a shield that provided some protection from the current. None of that was unusual for those fortunate enough to reach a time of life when youth was long ago, but this was much more than a normal phase of those who make such a journey through as many years as Eli Jared had traveled.

Now the physical evidences of memories were under threat as the new government had ordered pictures or records of those things that were photographed or recorded before July 16 to be destroyed. Eli Jared hid his pictures and letters in an old green ammunition box and buried it outside the Washington, D.C. condominium building in which he lived, confident that even if the box was discovered and destroyed, the revolutionaries would not find the times that were locked more securely in his mind. After all, they would not be able to find Eli Jared in the hide-a-way across the Potomac where on this day his hair was even grayer than before, his gray three-piece suit was more worn than before, and his times of green were now so distant they seemed to be the life of another person.

In one of his jacket pockets was a small plastic packet containing one cyanide capsule. That was a common item of most Americans by this time. It started seven years before this day; the capsule carried first by Americans who traveled overseas, to swallow in case they were captured by Islamist revolutionary terrorists to prevent the carrier from being tortured beyond endurance. Soon even non-traveling Americans started carrying them because the Islamist terrorists had come out of hiding, largely from sleeper-cells in Michigan and then in Minnesota and then throughout any number of major urban areas in the United States, committing the same captures and tortures and beheadings that had been performed with such consistency in other countries.

The small cyanide containers were first bought in horror, but soon the packages became so widespread that they were carried in the casual way in which men carried combs and women carried lipstick. Competing manufacturers used television commercials to sell their own versions, one called "Safeguard," another called "My Way," and another called "Contingency."

First there came suicide bombers in the United States entering shopping centers, restaurants, theaters and other public facilities. Magnetometers and pat-downs became common for security throughout the country.

Eli Jared knew that it was the way of the world for cultures to change and traditions to change and customs to change and mores to change and arts to change and even the polity to change, but never did he imagine a change of such immensity. This was the prologue to a new kind of life.

And today it had gone beyond prologue:

One year ago from today came the numerous devastations of areas in municipalities of the United States and Great Britain and selected cities of other countries with most attacks accomplished by terrorists wearing shaheed belts; by improvised explosive devices; by takeovers of airliners; and in later months by missiles armed with chemical, biological, and nuclear warheads.

Instead of devastation, France, Germany and Belgium encountered an endless stream of Islamic Revolutionaries, some of them residents, some of them invaders, and all three nations fell in days. While some organized underground movements, the revolutionaries were met by others with white flags and even some cheers as they paraded yelling "Death to America" in one language or another.

Uniquely, not one city in the People's Republic of China was attacked or invaded.

Many, but not all Moslem countries were left untouched. Islamic governments that did not support the revolution were considered to be "subversives" and "treasonous counter-revolutionaries." Malaysia's government was on the list of counter-revolutionary nations and so the Petronas Twin Towers in Kuala Lumpur were destroyed in the same way the New York towers of the World Trade Center had been destroyed years earlier. The government of Malaysia was quickly replaced by trusted revolutionaries with its former elected government executed in a public spectacle held in the Stadium Nasional in Bukit Jalil's sports complex.

Brunei, whose Sultan opposed the revolutionaries, was left with no more than a few standing buildings, the Sultan's fate a mystery.

Then the United States became the area of concentration in a sudden and surprising coordination of sleeper-cells that surfaced throughout the country all at once.

U.S. Armed Forces were still fighting back despite the urging of the revolutionaries to all members of the U.S. military below the highest-ranking officers to surrender themselves and their weapons in return for amnesty. The highest ranking officers were exempt from the offer and instead would "receive justice." Casualties on both sides were so immense and wide-spread and occurred so quickly that neither side had the time or ability to give an estimate. The revolutionaries achieved their objective with the fall of the District of Columbia on July the 16th.

In D.C. the revolutionaries captured and beheaded countless U.S. government workers; some had been elected, some appointed, some were careerists, and the victors dragged their bodies tied to the bumpers of automobiles, driving them through the city on Pennsylvania Avenue, Constitution Avenue, Independence Avenue, and up 14th Street in front of stunned people. Some of the children applauded, not quite comprehending the difference between reality and a movie.

The changing of names was immediate: the Washington Monument was now known as the Monument of the Jihad; the White House was now called the Grand Palace of the Islamic Fundamentalist Republic of America (IFRA) where the leader of the revolutionary government, Hashem al-Awadhi was in residence, and Pennsylvania Avenue was now Medina Avenue. Down Medina Avenue from the Grand Palace of the IFRA, the Council of Guardians was given a place for assembly in what had been the U.S. Capitol Building.

There was a call issued through all media for the young and other able-bodied to volunteer for renovation projects:

The exterior of what had been known as the Jefferson Memorial was to have the words Allah Akbar etched around its dome, and under the dome, the statue of Thomas Jefferson would be removed, replaced with the standing marble likeness of Abd al-Jabad.

What had been the short life of the World War II Monument was to be excavated and called the Gallery of Mullahs with fifty-six statues of the heroes who led the victory of the revolution.

The statue of President Abraham Lincoln within the Lincoln Memorial would be destroyed and the shell of the Memorial would be used to house a sitting statue of Majid Omar al-Anqari.

Across the river, Arlington Cemetery would be bulldozed into a park for the leisure of men; the old gravestones used to construct public latrines. There would be a playground for boys directly over what had been the Kennedy gravesite. The Eternal Flame had already been extinguished.

All Sundays were to have their mornings reserved for the public to come to the Ellipse to witness executions for Crimes Against the State, including the stoning to death of women who were adulterers, and other women receiving the lesser punishment of being shot in the back of the head if they were guilty of other offenses against strict Sharia law. Others who would be publicly executed on Sundays on the Ellipse were Moslem men and women who were known to have opposed the Jihad, and considered themselves Americans who believed in Islam but did not believe in the fundamentalism that won the war.

On July the 16th every television channel and radio station had the same message, labeled as Mullah Mostafa Jahangiri's proclamation to the people: "I greet all residents on behalf of the Islamic Fundamentalist Republic of America. National Day will be commemorated on the Mall of the capital city on every July the 16th, celebrating the victory of your Revolutionaries. Another day of jubilation will be celebrated every September the 11th in recognition of the successful attacks that led to our victory."

He went on to say, "The authority belongs exclusively to Allah.

No others, no matter who they may be, have the right to govern on any basis other than the authority that has been conferred by Allah. It is the religious expert and no one else who should occupy himself with the affairs of government. He should implement punishments just as the Prophet Mohammad did, and he should rule according to Allah's revelation. We want a ruler who would cut off the hand of his own son if he steals, and would flog and stone his near relative if that relative fornicates." That was a direct repeat of what the Ayatollah Ruhollah al-Musavi al-Khomeini had said in 1970, nine years before his successful takeover of Iran, creating the first Islamic Revolutionary Fundamentalist Government in the world.

The Mullah's proclamation concluded with the order that on the following day at 9:11 a.m. the designation of the current calendar would be changed to the year 1450 of the Islamic Hijra calendar that began with Mohammed's emigration from Mecca to Medina.

The city Eli Jared knew as home was now called the District of the Revolution. That night he started the lonely and dangerous journey out of the city. He was a recognizable figure. He did not pray for safety for fear his appeal would mix with so many others in prayer that night, making those with dependents more difficult for God to hear. Eli Jared had no dependents and was clearly aware that he had already lived a full life. But even without prayer Eli Jared reached his destination without becoming another casualty. Maybe God heard Eli Jared's thoughtful absence of prayer. Whether that was true or untrue, his life was not yet full enough, because it was to become more filled than he could ever had prophesied.

CHAPTER

2

In the Shelter

IT WAS AFTER midnight, Sunday having passed to Monday, and across the Potomac the lamps in a room of the apartment building were on, illuminating the old man who was joined by young Angus Glass whose shaking voice said, "They won, Mr. Jared! How did they do it, sir?"

Eli Jared's tall frame was apparent even though he was seated. Unmistakable was that distinguished face with a thin gray mustache that the nation had seen for so many years. His wearing of a vest enhanced that eminence. The only visual interruption in his look of importance was one of his strange idiosyncrasies: he was wearing an eye-patch on a thin black piece of elastic that wrapped around his head and the elastic strap was now holding the eye-patch against Eli Jared's forehead. Sometimes he had it over his left eye and sometimes, for no apparent reason he had it right above his nose, but usually he had it higher. He stared at the young man. Eli

Jared was in no mood to be in the company of some immature bureaucrat who wanted some words of security. Then he surrendered to all the courtesy he could muster. "Sit down, sit down. Take that chair."

Angus Glass nodded, and then sat opposite Eli Jared with a small coffee table between them in an apartment that was luxurious except for the lack of windows. But even if the apartment had windows the sky would not be in sight. The apartment was in a building next to other apartment buildings without windows and across the street from office buildings without windows and a hospital without windows and all kinds of buildings without windows that comprised the city beneath a mountain in Virginia. The city in the mountain was guarded by a massively tall and wide iron door covered with concrete in thickness of seven feet, so heavy that it took fourteen minutes to open or close. Closing with more speed was another barrier closer to the facility; this barrier included two gates, one rising from the ground, the other coming from above, the two clamping together to become a single entity. Beyond that barrier was a series of barricades that opened only when the others were closed. All of this was part of the Continuity of Government (COG) Facility that was built to execute the frequently updated document known as COOP, the Continuity of Operations Plan of the United States of America.

"Mr. Jared, do they have the President?" Angus Glass asked.

"The President isn't here yet."

"Then where is he? This is impossible to believe!"

"The President will be here," Eli Jared added with pretended knowledge of what was going on beyond the city in the mountain, bending to the role of security that Angus Glass expected of Eli Jared. And then the pretension was gone. "I don't know what happened at the White House. I don't know what prevents him from being here by now. I'm sorry." At his age, Eli Jared couldn't pretend anything for more than seconds of time. Conscience of honesty came much quicker than it did in earlier years.

Angus Glass generally felt stable and knowledgeable like most young men in government, but he did not feel stable or knowledgeable in the presence of Eli Jared who was his senior in life by decades and his senior in wisdom further than calendars could measure.

But Angus Glass never let the wisdom of others stand in his way. Tonight he was fidgeting in his chair, his thin frame never sitting still but moving forward and moving to one side and then the other, with his fingers clasping and opening, his eyes blinking too often. He faced Eli Jared who was as stone-like as the seated statue in the Lincoln Memorial, if it was still there. "Mr. Jared, do you know how they did it? How could they have done it?"

Eli Jared looked down at his own hands resting on the arms of his chair and he mumbled something. It was inaudible.

"What was that, sir?"

Eli Jared looked into the eyes of Angus Glass. He still talked softly but it wasn't a mumble. "I said, 'hogwash.'"

For as long as he could, Angus Glass said nothing in response as he tried to figure out what Eli Jared meant. But he soon gave up. "Hogwash, sir?"

"What happened, Mr. Glass, is that we were washing hogs while our enemies were planning our defeat. The terrorist cells in the United States were taking advantage of our never-ending debates on what we called profiling and diversity and the right of privacy to the exclusion of finding out all we had access to find out. And while all this hogwash was going on, recruitment for terrorist cells in the United States flourished. In time there become more and more cells than we ever thought could be established, and with increasing memberships. We prevented ourselves from knowing names and numbers of members or locations of cells or the preparations of their plan. And when their overseas leaders felt the numbers were high enough and the locations were spread wide enough and the plan was prepared enough, they ordered a scheduled date at a scheduled time. It wasn't the first time they scheduled attacks but with so many successes behind them with weaknesses and strengths now known, this was being organized on a more massive scale than ever before. We called them sleeper-cells, but when the day and time came the cells were all wide awake and we were the sleepers, weren't we?"

Angus Glass cleared his throat, brushed his thin blonde hair back and said, "I thought if we lost the war it would mean more wars in the Mideast. Maybe a lot of wars in the Mideast. But not here. There have always been wars over there; thousands of years of wars; sect against sect, country against country, religion against religion, isn't that true?" And without waiting for an answer he went on. "That's what the Mideast has been and that's all I thought our defeat would mean: more wars over there. I never thought there would be a takeover of our country, did you, sir?"

Rudeness and impatience, like conscience, also came quickly to Eli Jared as it did to most of those living in advanced age. "Of course I did. Of course it meant a takeover of the United States. As you said, Mr. Glass, defeat would mean more wars in the Mideast, but this time what you and your ilk didn't want to think deeply enough to discover was the obvious: Those new wars would only be a pathway to an objective our enemies never disguised. Didn't you hear them? Didn't you hear them announce their destination? Didn't you hear the three words that were stated and chanted and shouted every day since 9-11? No. I'm wrong. It started years before 9-11. Three words recited in one way or another every day: 'Death to America!'

How did you miss those words, son? Deaf? You and your ilk deaf? I heard them. What did you do? Cover your ears?"

Angus Glass was a convenient and necessary target, providing an outlet for all the fury that was locked inside Eli Jared. Angus Glass was merely the victim of that fury created by the horror that was occurring beyond the walls of the shelter. That victim was uncomfortable from the new attitude of anger displayed by Eli Jared. His answer was only to give another shift in his sitting position.

Eli Jared stared at the shift of Angus Glass and drilled it in by saying, "Huh? Huh? Huh?"

This time there was a fast response. "I don't know, sir."

"'Death to America!' Did you hear them?"

"Yes."

"What did you think? Did you think they didn't mean it?"

"I don't know what I thought, sir. I thought it was just—just the kind of thing they said. Like a phrase. Like a slogan."

"We would still have a country if you and your ilk just got the wax out of your ears!"

"Yes, sir," Angus Glass agreed quickly. He so much wanted to appear as an equal to Eli Jared but he simply didn't know how to do it. He tried silence for a while and then he nodded although Eli Jared didn't ask him anything but it could appear as though he was still thinking about getting the wax out of his ears and the ears of his ilk. After the nod he pointed to nothing in particular and then withdrew his hand, assuming the motion somehow gave a signal in advance that he was about to change the subject. "What do we do now, sir?"

Eli Jared took the bait. He wanted to take the bait. "We wait."

"What do we wait for, sir?"

"We wait—we wait—we wait and then we have to do—what we have to do."

"Yes, sir."

"Our error, Mr. Glass, was in not doing what was necessary when we were the master of events. We waited until we were the slave of events."

"Yes, sir."

"You listening?"

"Yes, sir."

"You listening?"

"Yes, sir, I am listening."

"That's true of people, too, isn't it?"

"What's that, sir?"

"Slaves. They're slaves because they put off doing what they should have done when they were the masters. Right?"

"Okay."

"True of people and so we should have known it was true of nations. Get it? People and nations feel elevated by not interfering with their short-range sense of morality. That always guarantees a later chain on their ankles at best—and where we are today at worst."

"Yes sir, but if I may—what is it that we have to do—what we have to do? That's what you said; that we have to do what we have to do."

"Fight back. No matter what, we have to fight back. If, God willing, President Wadsworth is alive and is able, then under his leadership, we will make the moments into what Winston Churchill would have rallied us to do. That is, if there is any Churchillian strength left in the President."

"Could President Wadsworth be in the air somewhere?"

Eli Jared actually thought about it. He had heard so much of his own voice that just thinking had a calming effect on him. "He could be. Yes. Yes, he could be. He could be on a Doomsday Plane."

"What's that, sir?"

"A plane."

"It's an airplane for—doomsday?"

"There's a contingency for everything. And tonight is everything. When the Doomsday Planes aren't in use they're at Andrews Air Force Base in waiting and staffed and being maintained and on alert and ready to move at all times."

"Did you make that plural? There are more than one?"

"There's a contingency for everything. There's a contingency for a contingency."

"Do you think he's on one of them?"

"There's no way for me to know. But if he is on a Doomsday Plane, then he knows where we are. We're monitored on that plane, you know, as well as everyone in the line of succession."

"How can that be?"

"It can be."

"Mr. Jared, can you answer what may seem like a naïve question? Mr. Jared, who are 'we'?"

Eli Jared clamped his lips together signaling his despair at the question. "We are Sebotus, Mr. Glass."

"Sebotus?"

It was unfortunately apparent that Angus Glass did not know what Eli Jared was talking about, giving reason for Eli Jared to reach the limit of his patience toward the young bureaucrat. "What do you think you're doing here?"

"I knew this was the place I was to get to in case of emergency. I was told I couldn't bring anyone with me and I couldn't tell anyone about this place, not even my wife if I had one. I don't have one so that didn't mean anything to me personally. All I know is I was given the pass and the briefing and I had a tour through here."

"That's all you know?"

"That's about it, sir."

Eli Jared breathed in and exhaled in a long sigh, which was his habit before going into an explanation of something that he felt should already be known by whoever he was addressing. "Sebotus means the Surviving Executive Branch of the United States. Inside of this underground city are some thousand or so people. Maybe more. I don't know. They work here in ninety-day shifts. They aren't a part of Sebotus; they aren't part of the Surviving Executive Branch of the United States, but they maintain this facility. Staff. They're staff. There is someone from every craft imaginable from cooks to a brain surgeon. Maybe not a brain surgeon. I don't know what he is. And there is also an administrative staff. Different combinations of them hold parts of the protocol that, in a contingency like this one, are combined. The protocol is the Continuity of Operations Plan. President Wadsworth wrote the current one. It contains a list. It tells who composes the new Executive Branch if the original members are missing."

"You mean if they're dead?"

"Dead or unable to contact this facility."

"Do you think I'm on that list of the new Executive Branch?"

"You're on it. You got in here, didn't you?"

"Yes. Sure."

"You came here by military helicopter, didn't you?"

"I did, sir."

"From the White House South Lawn or the Pentagon?"

"I live in Roslyn. I went to the Pentagon."

"And you have the digital pass or you would never have been able to leave the Pentagon and you would never have been able to enter this place without it. Right? You performed all the prescribed functions at the barriers here. Right?"

"Yes, sir."

"You weren't permitted to bring anyone or anything in with you other than your pass and the clothes you were wearing. Am I right? Everything else confiscated; not just metal—even a piece of paper with anything written on it, even your wallet, even your currency, even your gum. Right?"

"Yes, sir. I didn't have any gum, sir. I don't chew it."

"That's nice. What's your job in the administration?"

"I'm an Assistant Secretary of Housing and Urban Development."

"You're very likely going to cross out the word 'Assistant.' If Secretary Lawrence doesn't get here it would be very surprising if you won't be the *Secretary* of Housing and Urban Development."

"I will?"

For a moment he sounded fatherly. "You will, son." Then he added a quick and sarcastic, "Congratulations."

"What will I do as Secretary of Housing and Urban Development here—in this facility?"

"Build houses for the poor, I suppose. Frankly, I can't think of anything for you to do. That's your problem. Too bad, you won't have any staff to speak of, but you'll be promoted alright. Secretary Lawrence must like you, God knows why. You're the one Lawrence obviously recommended to the President. That's why you're part of Sebotus. Weren't you ever told anything at all about what would be expected of you, should this happen?"

"I never even heard the word, 'Sebotus.'"

"Oh, for God's sake."

"They never said that. At least I don't think so."

"It wasn't always called that. There's been a progression of Executive Orders that created all this since Dwight David Eisenhower was president. You ever heard of him?"

"Of course. Of course I heard of him. The general."

"Good. Good. Good for you. The idea of an emergency executive branch of government has changed in directives, in organization, and even in location over and over again during the years, but its foundation has remained the same. The main item that has remained the same is that members of Sebotus serve at the pleasure of the president, and if there is no president we follow the list of succession—and then it was decided to even go beyond the list of succession. And even beyond—beyond. Then there's a plan for a return to constitutional rule, and that's the way it's written."

"Mr. Jared. You aren't with the government now, are you?"

For once, Eli Jared was silent. Then in a softer voice he said, "No. I hold no position anymore. I haven't for years."

"Then why are you here, sir?"

"President Wadsworth wanted me here." Then, in a louder voice, "Is that alright with you, son?"

Angus Glass nodded. "Yes sir, of course. But if the President isn't alive, then what happens?"

"You know the answer to that. Then the Vice President will run the government."

"I hesitate to ask—but he isn't here either, is he, Mr. Jared?"

"Maybe he's on one of the Doomsday Planes—with the President."

"Mr. Jared, what if neither of them is alive—neither the President nor the Vice President?"

"There are seventeen more people in the line of succession."

"And if none of them get here? How long do we wait for one of the seventeen? Do you know how long we wait?"

Eli Jared looked at his watch. "About ten hours from now. I can't figure it out. You're the smart one. What's ten hours from now?"

"You know that? You know that we'll know in ten hours?"

"I know that."

"And then what?"

"We may see the 'then what.' Until then all we can do is be patient."

"What if all of them have been captured—the whole line of succession—what if they've all been captured or are dead?"

"Then, Mr. Glass," and he leaned toward Angus Glass and spoke very quietly. "and then there are us."

Angus Glass's eyes enlarged and his mouth opened and for a few seconds no words came out although his mouth was in a perfectly poised position to say something. Apparently he finally caught on. When he regained his ability to talk, he offered his assessment. "Holy Horsefeathers!"

That was when a feminine voice came from the loudspeakers in the room. "Attention all members of the Sebotus. The Secretary of Commerce has arrived. Secretary of Commerce Desmond has arrived in the COG Facility."

Eli Jared put his hands together and clenched them hard against each other. He stared at his hands as he tightened their clasp even more. "Thank you, God." Then he unclasped them, stood up, and looked sharply at Angus Glass. Now that he was standing, it was apparent that his tall and stately frame was also slightly bent, perhaps with some pain but most likely out of habit. "We have a president," he said. "We have a president from the line of succession. Thank God. Get to your apartment, son. I'm going to see if I can visit with the Secre—with the President of the United States." He walked toward the door.

"Mr. Jared?" came Angus Glass's very quiet voice.

Eli Jared turned his head to face Angus Glass. "Yes?"

"May I go with you, sir? I would like to meet him."

Eli Jared continued his walk to the door, opened it, and then looked back at Angus Glass with an expression that indicated it was painful to look at him. "No, Mr. Glass. That would not be appropriate." That statement was the ultimate of self-discipline. What he restrained himself from saying was that he wouldn't think of burdening the new president with such a meeting. However he did add, "This is not the time or place for a courtesy call."

Eli Jared must have cared a great deal about the coming meeting with Matt Desmond. He moved the eye-patch from his forehead down to carefully cover his left eye.

CHAPTER

3

The Oath

EVEN AT TIMES of extreme importance—times of life or death; of peace or war; of the determination of whether all civilization will be victorious or defeated—there is a pretty woman. Always. They come out of nowhere. They somehow come out of the walls. Even iron walls covered with concrete.

And so there was Traci Howe. Naturally.

She met him in the hallway. "Mr. Jared, I'm Traci Howe with the staff here. Secretary Desmond asked to see you."

"I was just going to see him. I heard the announcement."

"But first Rear Admiral Keith Kaylin wants to meet with you before going in."

"Who's he?"

"He flew the Secretary here. He's part of the Sebotus. Not staff, not workforce, but part of the Sebotus itself—like you. He's representing the Chairman of the Joint Chiefs of Staff in General

Ostan's absence. As of this morning I've been assigned to him. Right now he's in the reception room outside the Succession Apartments three floors down. He'll bring you to Secretary Desmond. I'm to bring you to Rear Admiral Kaylin."

"Thank you, but you don't need to bother, Miss. I can go to the reception room. I know where it is. It's alright."

"But I'm supposed to take you there, Mr. Jared."

Eli Jared smiled and nodded. "Fine. Fine. I'd rather have you escort me than have Angus Glass as an escort."

She smiled. "Thank you, Mr. Jared."

To Eli Jared she was little more than a child but it was difficult not to notice her perfect posture, her short blonde hair, her appropriate dress in a blue skirt and sweater, and her calmness, as pretended as it might be, as she acted like an experienced guide through emergencies. All of that made her as pleasant to walk with as it would have been for him had he still been twenty years old. The great difference between those years and these years was that the word "future" regarding a pretty young woman was simply out of the question for too many reasons for any old man to enumerate. But nothing; not age or even wisdom, makes prettiness of woman insignificant. "Somehow I think you have received higher compliments than being compared to Angus Glass." Not an arguable observation.

Her smile went even wider. Her teeth were perfect.

This could be the end of the world, and he noticed she had good teeth. Is there no end to God's little provocations, even at moments of such crisis?

Rear Admiral Kaylin looked exactly what anyone named Rear Admiral Kaylin should look like; cleanly shaved, in a pressed uniform with short, well-combed black hair, matched by mirror-like polished black shoes. And when he stood for the entrance of Eli Jared escorted by Traci Howe, his height was almost startling. Eli Jared who was a tall man himself, had to look up at Admiral Kaylin, and Traci Howe might just as well have been looking at the ceiling.

The reception room obviously served multiple functions as it had a large oak table in its center and eight chairs on each side with one chair at each end. Electronic and digital devices, big and small, were on the table. Traci Howe introduced Admiral Kaylin to Eli Jared, they shook hands, and Traci unfortunately left the room.

"Sit down, sir," Admiral Kaylin said as his hand gestured toward the head of the table. Eli Jared nodded; sat where Admiral Kaylin indicated, and Admiral Kaylin sat at the table to Eli Jared's right. "Mr. Jared, I flew Secretary Desmond in. You should know he was highly panicked when I got to him. He was in his basement."

Eli Jared clenched his lips together and nodded. "That's a reasonable place for him to have been, Admiral. I can understand how he would have been panicked. I'm panicked, too. We're all panicked. We're all panicked, aren't we?"

"I used the wrong word. I mean he's not in good shape."

"How bad?"

"He's not quite right, sir."

"You mean he's nuts?"

Admiral Kaylin wanted to be careful and diplomatic in the terms he used but since Eli Jared was so blunt, he surrendered to clarity: "That's what I mean, Mr. Jared."

"Nuts?" He wanted the Admiral to say it.

"Nuts, Mr. Jared. Truly nuts."

"Are you an M.D., Admiral?"

"No, sir."

There was a sudden spurt of courtesy in Eli Jared. "I'm not asking that in criticism. I just want to know."

"I realize that, sir."

"Why couldn't it simply be shock? Maybe the man was temporarily in shock. Could anyone blame him? Good Lord, there he was like all of us, multiplied by the fact that he was in the line of succession for the presidency. Just shock. Temporary. That's all."

"Maybe it is. But it just—Secretary Desmond is a fine man, I know that, but I'm concerned that he can't function well, that he can't really—"

"Be president? You mean he can't handle the presidency now?"

"That's right, sir, but 'now' is such an extraordinary period of time and we don't know how long it will last. If he reacted as he has, how can he handle the kinds of things that will come up during a period of presidency—particularly under the conditions? Mr. Jared, it's really bad. You'll see. I feel that we simply can't let him become president, Mr. Jared. I'm asking you to discourage him, sir, because it is out of the question by any criterion of common sense."

"It's not up to me, Admiral."

"For all we know, it might be up to you, sir. He said he wanted to see you. He respects you. Everyone in D.C. does, sir, and you know that. He knows your history, and he knows you're President Wadsworth's best friend. That means something in itself. He knows what you have done from your military service forward through when you were our Ambassador to the U.N.—before the U.N. committed suicide—and National Security Advisor and—he's awed by you."

The inner door swung open and Secretary Desmond stood in the doorway. His gray hair, what little there was of it, was disheveled and his plaid shirt was untucked, hanging unceremoniously well below his waist, in front of his denim pants. Both Eil Jared and Admiral Kaylin stood up.

"Jared? Jared? Come on in! Did you bring a Bible? I want the oath. I want a Judge. Don't we have to have a Judge? Jared, are you a Judge?"

Eli Jared hesitated and then shook his head and said softly, "No," and he hesitated and then said, "No, Mister Secretary, I'm not a Judge."

"Come on in my office here, Jared. Come on in and let's get this oath-thing done with. You're a Judge. You're everything else aren't you? You should know how to do it. You can be my Sarah Hughes. Remember? She was the judge who gave the oath-thing to LBJ. Well, wait. Wait. Wait a minute. Let me get cleaned up. Someone ought to take a picture. You in the uniform—you got a camera? Give me ten minutes to get cleaned up, and then you, Jared, you give me the oath-thing and you," he said pointing at Admiral Kaylin, "you get a picture of it. Get a picture. Like they got of LBJ on *Air Force One* at Love Field in Dallas. You wouldn't know. You weren't born then. Or get someone in the hallway to take the picture. Anybody. Then you won't have to take it. You in uniform will look good in the picture. Get someone in here and you can be in the picture, too. Anyone can take the thing. You can be in the background like Al Thomas or Jack Valenti was. They weren't in flight then, you know. So neither am I." Secretary Desmond turned around and walked back in his apartment, slamming the door shut.

Eli Jared exchanged a look with Admiral Kaylin. Eli Jared's expression said all there was to say. Even if Admiral Kaylin *was* an M.D., such a credential would not be necessary to make a diagnosis in this case.

"Do you see what I mean?" Admiral Kaylin asked, knowing his words had been proven.

"But on the other hand, there's nothing wrong with his memory, Admiral. He certainly remembers the details of what happened on *Air Force One* when President Johnson took the oath of office. I don't remember those details."

"Who cares, sir? I don't mean to be disrespectful but I remember the argyle pattern of my socks when I was three years old. But he doesn't seem to have memory of important things. Besides his absurd remarks, he hasn't asked one question about what's going on in the country during this unbelievably unthinkable time and he hasn't asked about his wife or his children or his grandchildren. And he isn't acting the way he acted at Commerce. I knew him very well at Commerce. We in the Joint Chiefs work closely with Secretary of Defense Miller and he and Secretary Desmond served together in the Gavin Administration and got to know each other at cabinet meetings and other things; receptions and dinners and things. They became very close. So I got to know him, too, through Miller. There was nothing wrong with Desmond. He's a fine man. He's a devoted husband and family-man. We've known each other, talked together, laughed together, traveled together a number of times for the last three, four years, and now all he calls me is the man in uniform."

"I'm afraid he's your Commander in Chief."

"Not yet, sir."

"Yes he is. He is your Commander in Chief, Admiral. He's Acting President of the United States of America."

"He hasn't taken the oath yet, Mr. Jared."

"He doesn't need to take the oath. He's President by virtue of the fact that he's next in line for the presidency until someone gets here or contacts us who's higher up in succession, if that ever comes. We're just going to have to work with him."

"But if he's—nuts?" He chose to use Eli Jared's word. "Is there no way around it? Mr. Jared, common sense dictates he's in no shape to be president."

"I don't know. I don't know." He thought for a while with Admiral Kaylin staring at him. Then in a quiet and unemotional tone he said, "There *is* a constitutional provision; the Twenty-Fifth

Amendment about declaring a president incompetent. I can't think of what it says. But that's easy enough to find out. There are constitutions all over this place. I think the amendment calls for the Vice President and cabinet officers and some congressional leaders, none of whom are here, to be involved in the declaration that the president is nuts—incompetent. I don't think it says anything about a situation like this when none of those people are around. A situation like this was never addressed."

"So he's president right now?"

"Check!"

"Tell him he has to take the oath and there isn't any judge around to administer it. Let's take advantage of the fact that he doesn't think he's acting president until he gets that oath."

"I can't do that. I can't start lying. I suppose I could say that it has to be done with his hand on the Bible and I can tell him I don't have a Bible. But I do. They have one in my drawer. And besides he'll find one. There's one in a drawer in the desk of every one of these apartments. In fact, I believe there's a U.S. Constitution in each apartment, too. I don't want to lie. Maybe it's just that I don't want to be caught. I'm thinking too quick."

"May I suggest that you take the Bible out of his apartment drawer, sir?"

"No." And then he added, "No, no, no. God would kill me for that before I even have an opportunity to die. If I have to die now I want to die with His grace; not His disgust."

"Lie to Desmond, sir! Tell him whatever lies you *have* to tell him."

"How many lies do you want me to tell the poor soul?"

"A dozen. Two dozen. One hundred. One thousand if necessary. If one million lies will save the nation, wouldn't you tell them, sir?"

"Save the nation? I'm not sure it even exists. We just have to work around him."

"How do we do that?"

"I'll figure out a way. We have to think."

The inner door swung open again, and there was the world's highest hope of mankind once more standing in the doorway. This time his hair was wet and combed, his plaid shirt was tucked into his denim pants, and he was obviously all ready to be photographed just like LBJ. "Sarah?" he said to Eli Jared, "Sarah Hughes, get in here! And you too, Valenti! So now you're in the armed forces. That's good. That will look good. Get someone in the hallway to take the picture."

"Sir," Admiral Kaylin said to President Desmond, "before doing that, we better take care of what is always administered to a new president."

"What's that, Valenti?"

"A physical, sir. That's part of the procedure and we should do it by the book, sir; by the Constitution: a physical, a judge, a Bible, and there's an amendment about a photograph. But the physical comes first, sir. That's why they have a hospital in this facility. Every president has to get a physical before taking office. Ever since George Washington, sir."

Eli Jared was staring at Admiral Kaylin, amazed at his acting ability combined with his most absurd recitation of constitutional law.

In contrast, Matt Desmond was impressed with what he assumed was Admiral Kaylin's knowledge. "Did LBJ get a physical? Where? Over at Parkland Hospital?"

"Yes, sir. Over at Parkland Hospital. That's right."

Matt Desmond looked over at Eli Jared who was still staring at Admiral Kaylin in bewilderment. "Is that right, Sarah?"

At first, Eli Jared didn't recognize that Secretary Desmond was talking to him as no one had ever addressed him as 'Sarah' before.

"Sarah! For God's sake, Sarah, is that right?"

Now Eli Jared turned to Secretary Desmond and quickly figured out how to answer him. He gave a slight rotation of his head but it wasn't a nod or a shake. It wasn't much of anything. "Jack Valenti here should know the procedure, sir."

"Then let's do it! Let's get the fool thing over with. Let's stick to the Constitution before they impeach me. We're not going to let the congress say I took the office unconstitutionally. Those hair-brains in the congress are just waiting to impeach me. We'll stick to the Constitution and give some doctor my blood and urine and all that, and he can tell the congress I did the whole thing constitutionally. Then they can all go sulk. Let's go, Valenti. You come with us, Sarah."

CHAPTER

4

The Protocols

"THEY'RE GOING TO kill him!" Angus Glass almost yelled it out over his breakfast of pancakes, bacon, hashbrown potatoes and orange juice in the crowded Sebotus Cafeteria.

"Shhhh," Traci Howe put her index finger to her lips, and then she said very softly, with her eyes looking like giant blue saucers in visual response to the statement of Angus Glass, "Everyone is so jumpy! Cool it. We're all supposed to be cool. Now—are you sure?"

Angus Glass lowered his voice almost to a whisper. "They're going to kill him. I know it." But then the volume of his voice increased. "I just know it."

"Shhhh! Why? Why would they do that? And who are 'they'?" She put a fork into the slice of watermelon in her fruit plate.

He lowered the volume of his voice again. "Because they don't want him to be president."

"But who are 'they'? Who doesn't want him to be president?"

"A lot of the Sebotus. Everyone in Sebotus wants to be president."

"You think?"

"You bet I do."

"Do you want to be president, Angus?"

"No. And even if I did, I wouldn't kill anyone to be president. I saw them bring Secretary Desmond to the hospital last night. He isn't out of there yet. For all we know, he's dead. And he's the President, Traci! Let's call him what he is. They're killing President Desmond! They want it to get to the Shadow Government without anyone in the legal succession left alive. I mean we're talking about the presidency!"

"I don't believe that."

"I bet you that—"

Angus Glass was interrupted by an announcement from the familiar anonymous feminine voice on the loudspeakers: "Attention all members of Sebotus. All members please report to the Lucite Room in Building C-A at 10:00 a.m. The doors will close at 10:01. The only staff members who will be admitted are those with a T25 designation marked on their digital badges. Repeat: All Sebotus members please report to the Lucite Room in Building C-A at 10:00 a.m. The doors will close at 10:01. The only staff members who will be admitted are those with a T25 designation marked on their digital badges."

Traci stared at Angus. "That sounds important. Oh, God, Angus, pray. That sounds important."

"They're going to say that Desmond died in surgery. That's what they're going to say."

"How do you know? You're not telling me how you know, because you don't know. I just hope they don't announce that the revolutionaries are on their way here. Be real!" And she felt her nose was running and she quickly wiped above her lips with her napkin.

"My nose. I have allergies."

"Do you have family, Traci?"

"Mom and Dad are in Mexico. They left their home in Texas, in El Paso, and got to Juarez as soon as things started to happen. Most of the Sebotus staffers were able to give their people some warning. Not much, but some and most of them got to a safe place. Are your people okay?"

"My mother is in San Francisco. That's home. She's safe there. The revolutionaries will leave San Francisco alone. It's a sanctuary city."

"And your father?"

"I don't know. I don't even know him. They divorced when I was a kid—a baby—an infant. I never heard from him. I know what they're going to say at the meeting, Traci. I know. Desmond's dead. That's what they're going to say, but I'll bet they won't announce he's been killed!"

"You're a member of Sebotus. You'll be at the meeting and you'll find out." Out of nervousness rather than need, her left hand swept back her short cropped blonde hair in repeated gestures.

"Won't you be there?" Angus asked.

"I'm staff. I'm not T25 staff. I'm just lowly staff."

"What, exactly do you do every day here?"

"Whatever they tell me. I'm a Utility Girl. Isn't that what they call a baseball player who does anything? So when the Sebotus members were called I was assigned to Rear Admiral Kaylin. I'm sort of a secretary-—Girl-Friday for him."

"Is he good? You like him?"

"Oh, he's fine. He's a nice man. He wasn't my first choice but I like him. He's what you call 'a gentleman.' Who was assigned to you?"

"No one. I wasn't given an assistant or a secretary. No Utility Girl."

She extended the palms of her hand in mid-air. "Ha!" And then she withdrew her hands and she reached over to touch his arm. "Oh, excuse me."

"Why do you suppose I didn't get someone assigned to me?"

Traci raised her eyebrows and shook her head. "I don't know, Angus. Who knows?"

"Who was your first choice to be assigned to?"

"Eli Jared."

"Oh, no!"

"What do you mean, 'oh, no'?"

Angus shrugged. "He's a grumpy old man. "

"He's a great old man. And I think his grumpiness is cute. He just tests people. He has fun and you have to have fun when you're around him. He isn't sour like so many others around here."

"Are you saying 'like me'?"

"I didn't say that."

"Traci, you're loony."

"I'm not loony!"

"Yes, you are. You said he isn't sour, but he's as sour as anyone I've ever met."

"You don't understand anyone older than thirty-five years old. You're just a big kid. Anyway, I didn't get assigned to him. Helen did. And she wanted to be assigned to him just like I did."

"Then both of you are loons."

"Do you remember what President Wadsworth said about Eli Jared after the Red Sea War?"

"Yeah."

"*What* then? What did he say?"

"I don't know."

"He said, 'He has the vision of an eagle that can see to every horizon and spot everything beneath him. He has the scent of a bloodhound that can sniff signs of both danger and peace. His sense of touch is like a manatee; the taste of a butterfly; and he can hear like a dolphin. And with it all he has the sixth sense of a cat. He is an American treasure.'"

"And he has the grumpiness of a dinosaur. And you're weird remembering all that. Traci, I can't go along with this. I can't go along with Sebotus. I should never have accepted being a part of it but I didn't really get what the whole thing meant. Coming out here by helicopter—being told of a secret shadow government in waiting. I felt, and I still feel that we can't just establish a secret government like this or we're no better than an invader, isn't that right? I mean that's not acting with principle."

"It isn't?"

"You bet it isn't. I mean, why didn't we have an emergency government elected? Why didn't we have one elected before all of this happened? Out in the open. A government of the people, by the people, and for the people. I despise secretiveness in what is supposed to be an open society. We should have elected a stand-by government years ago for an emergency. That would have been the moral way. Out in the open. Why didn't we do it that way? A stand-by government by free election. That's my principle. We should all have principles. Officers elected by the people to serve in that stand-by government. Why didn't we do that?"

"You know why we didn't?"

"Sure I know why. Because the people would have voted for better people than we have in this building right now."

"You're one of them in this building right now."

"I don't care."

"Oh, Angus. You're such a nice person who is so pitiful." She surprised herself by being that frank but she wasn't sorry she said it. "Whether or not they would have voted for better people isn't the reason they—and you—weren't elected."

"Then what is?"

"Because your head would now be decapitated from your body if your name had been made public in an election. You would have space between your head and your body. I don't know which of the two pieces would contain your principles, but I think it's in the middle part of your lower part. And so would every other member of the Sebotus be dead if their names were made public through an election."

He grunted.

"Don't you think?"

"There's got to be a better way with some iota of principle. There has to be a moral way." And then he added, "I just don't like what's being done. And I think your God, Eli Jared, is behind it. He isn't God, you know."

"And you're the smart one, Angus?"

"Yeah. That's right."

"I think you're jealous. He's everything you aren't, Angus Glass. I'm sorry to say that but it's time you grew up. You know, I have never heard Mr. Jared calling his beliefs 'his principles.' I suppose that's because people who have principles don't have to say they have them. Why don't you obey what you so ardently call your principles, Angus Glass? Come on. You can walk out of here. I'll make sure they open the doors to let you out. Leave your pass behind with me. I'm cleared to receive anyone's pass."

Angus Glass shook his head. "Come on, come on, come on. No, I'm not going outside. You know very well that if I left here I'd be killed by the lunatics out there. I'm not crazy."

"Your morality is becoming very hard to follow."

He didn't respond.

"Your morality is walking through a labyrinth. Turn around and walk back where you came in if you can still find all the right openings."

"Yeah."

"Oh, Angus, you're not even listening. You like to make grand statements about high-toned philosophies—and you probably believe them, or you think you do—but when it comes right down to it, when it's a matter of what could be your own life, you'll be part of the unelected secret emergency government, alright. You'll be part of it because you would choose to join what you loathe rather than risk your neck." And she put her straight index finger of her right hand in a horizontal movement across her neck from left to right while she made a gurgling noise from the back of her throat. "You have no principle that supersedes your own life. You better go and get ready, Angus. You better put on a tie. You don't want to be late and untidy for the Sebotus meeting—or for your jaunt outside—whichever one you choose. Remember I'm always here to accept your pass, and I'll always be willing to show you to the door. I'm a perfect hostess. I'm a Utility Girl."

"I don't need to get ready yet. There's time."

"I'm just giving you enough time to be alone so you can decide where you want to be at ten o'clock. Actually you have until 10:01 to be where your principles guide you. You better decide, don't you think?"

The doors of the Lucite Room didn't really close at 10:01. It was 10:03 when Matt Desmond came in, braced on Admiral Kaylin's arm. Everyone in the room stood up, and then the doors were closed. The room was very long and housed a conference table that seated eighteen and was made of transparent Lucite. The entire room was easily as luxurious as any corporation's board room. Once Matt Desmond and Admiral Kaylin were seated, the other participants sat back down with all chairs at the table filled, eight on each side of the table with one end of the table having its chair occupied by Matt Desmond. The chair at the other end of the table was occupied by a very stately and dignified woman probably in her late 50s, wearing a conservative brown suit with her almost-red hair tied behind her head. Each place at the table had a nameplate, tabletop microphones and a pocket-sized copy of the United States Constitution. Against the walls on both short sides of the room and one of the two long sides of the room, were chairs for other members of Sebotus and also top members of the staff of Sebotus.

The woman at one end of the table stood up again. "I'm Elizabeth Hadley, Secretary of the Surviving Executive Branch of the United States Government. Other than the T25 staffers, all of the rest of you have been appointed by President Wadsworth to be the nation's Surviving Executive Branch should disaster strike, and disaster has struck.

"First, a word to the staffers," and she turned her attention to a cluster of those sitting against one of the walls. "Each of you, please pick up some of the small white boxes in my adjoining office before leaving after the meeting. In them are networked digital desk calendars with signaled clocks. It is important they be placed in every occupied office in Sebotus during this emergency since without daylight and night, time passage soon becomes unknown and we should all be conscious of what day it is, what date it is, and what time it is. That data guides us when to sleep, to wake, to eat, and for those who take medications, when to take them. If you need more, see me as we have more. You and all others here in Sebotus may want to take advantage of the Mall for any change of clothes you may need. There is no cost. Simply return them when the emergency is over and you leave."

She turned her head back to those seated around the table. "Our communications with the outside world have been severely limited, more so than we ever envisioned, but our engineers, led by Ralph Ussery, believe we will have all communications up and running within the day. From our limited communications we can only confirm that the immediate events are not improving. You will receive current details when they are confirmed. The purpose of this meeting is to let you know that the protocols of the Continuity of Operations Plan have been opened.

"As you all know, only one of you at the table, the Secretary of Commerce, is on the list of presidential succession. Other than the Commerce Department, those at the table who worked directly for those in the line of succession will now fill the slots of all those who are on the list of succession but are not present. There are others here who are now Directors of some non-succession agencies and bureaus, some with special responsibilities as directed in advance by President Wadsworth. The only Sebotus staff present are T25, the designated ranking members of the staff.

"Before continuing with the protocols as called for in the Continuity of Operations Plan, I would like to turn the meeting over to Secretary Desmond."

It was noticed by everyone present that she did not refer to him as President Desmond. He stood up and in a very sad voice, all he said was, "I was born in Bermuda. Hamilton, Bermuda. My parents were British and our whole family came here after I was born. We went to Pennsylvania. Milwaukee, Pennsylvania." Then he sat down.

Immediately Admiral Kaylin talked into his tabletop microphone. "I'm Rear Admiral Keith Kaylin, United States Navy, member of Sebotus representing Chairman of the Joint Chiefs of Staff Ostan, and I have been with Secretary Desmond since he left D.C. last night. Prior to arrival, he was not well. Shortly after arrival, I brought him to the Sebotus Hospital. He's going to be just fine, but at present he is under some sedation. It should be known that last night at the hospital when we were gathering all the particulars, we asked Secretary Desmond to let us know his place and date of birth, and he volunteered to us that he was born in Hamilton, Bermuda and that he was naturalized when he was eighteen."

Elizabeth Hadley nodded. "Thank you, Admiral Kaylin. Unfortunately, as we all know, that means that constitutionally, Secretary Desmond is not in the line of succession As you all know, Bermuda was and remains a British Crown Colony.

"We are saddened that Secretary Desmond will not be able to assume the office of Acting President. He will remain Secretary of Commerce. That leaves the protocols of the Continuity of Government Plan, which in this case contains the advance emergency appointments by President Wadsworth in the naming of the Acting President and, in addition, the naming of all cabinet officers of the Executive Branch and his designated Directors of agencies and bureaus.

"The document, as required, is in the President's handwriting. He wrote this three weeks after his inauguration with some changes made more recently and initialed by the President. The changes were made due to deaths, retirements, resignations, and even changes of the President's mind since his original designations." She picked up the document in front of her and read from it: "Should all officers of the Executive Branch of the United States be detained or otherwise unable to fulfill their duties of office, I hereby nominate the Surviving Executive Branch of the United States (SEBOTUS) as specified in the Continuity of Government (COG) detailed in the Continuity of Operations Plan (COOP). If appropriate members of the congress are also detained or otherwise unable to fulfill their duties, the nominations for the Surviving Executive Branch of Government are automatically classified as appointments rather than nominees. In the later event of the presence of their superiors, the original pre-emergency appointment will immediately take effect. Those who are named to office in the emergency and retain that office throughout the emergency will serve until the return of constitutional government. During the emergency, their official titles of office will be preceded by the term 'Acting' with that term used on all documents. Obviously, if the Speaker of the House and/or the President Pro Tempore is/are accessible, they will take their prescribed place within the line of succession. As designated by me, James Wadsworth, President of the United States of America, those nominees or appointments in the Surviving Executive Branch of Government are as follows . . ."

She read the list one by one in a matter-of-fact tone with those named generally showing no acknowledgment other than a look of solemnity. Rear Admiral Keith Kaylin nodded slowly as he was named Acting Chairman of the Joint Chiefs of Staff. With the sole exception of Angus Glass, they all knew for a long time that should an emergency occur, they could be named to head the area of government in which they were appointed by the president, or they wouldn't have been asked by him to be part of the Sebotus. Angus Glass, with his mouth open, looked from side to side as different names were read, each time turning his head to stare at the one most recently named. When his own name was read he looked from side to side in quick spurts to see the reactions of the others who didn't care much who was going to be the Secretary of Housing and Urban Development.

Elizabeth Hadley then gave the oath of office to all of them as a group for which they stood with their right hands raised. She read the oath from her paper, and left only the office of Acting President of the United States and Acting Vice President of the United States to be named. She read further from President Wadsworth's paper, stating his choice for Acting Vice President of the United States as Leonard Mapes who he had also named as the Acting

National Security Advisor. She swore Leonard Mapes in for a second time.

The identity of the Acting President of the United States was no surprise to most of those at the meeting since he was the only one at the table who didn't currently work for the administration and was still left unassigned.

Elizabeth Hadley read, "Acting President of the United States shall be former U.S. Ambassador to the United Nations, Eli Jared."

Secretary of Commerce Desmond was one of the few who did not have that one figured out. On the announcement that Eli Jared would be acting president, Secretary Desmond lowered his brows, squinted and looked with anger at Elizabeth Hadley and then with the same expression stared at Eli Jared. Eli Jared stood and took the oath of office.

It all took place quickly, and to the added confusion of Secretary Desmond it was done without any of those present called by the name of Sarah Hughes or Al Thomas or Jack Valenti. And no one took photographs.

CHAPTER

5

Code of Conduct

DURING THE EARLY evening of Monday, July 17 every staff member of those serving the Sebotus members received a memorandum from Eli Jared titled "Code of Conduct":

MEMORANDUM TO: STAFF ONLY
FROM: ACTING PRESIDENT ELI JARED

The Acting Officers of the Surviving Executive Branch of the United States have been named on a document written previously by President Wadsworth. As Acting President of the United States I want you to know what is expected of you during these times. Much of this you already know because you were selected for your character, virtues, and talents. Beyond that, you have long rehearsed for such a contingency in which we now find ourselves. Regardless of that, I want you to re-read all that is vital for you to consistently keep in mind.

Your deportment is paramount. It may not be apparent every moment, but those of us who have been appointed by President Wadsworth look to you, the staff, for our own psychological well-being because you can make us weak or strong, anxious or calm, blundering or wise. Such responsibilities as you now have, come to very few. Seize them.

The most difficult mandatory rule here is that depression is forbidden. I apologize for giving such an unconstitutional order but under current events, Sebotus is not a democracy. If you ever feel you are on the verge of being unable to concentrate or unable to be pleasant to those around you, or if you feel you are losing a sense of values or your sense of humor, see me promptly. We will discuss the best thing for you to do. There are many options built into this system and into this facility. As you know, in this facility there is a Chapel, the Gymnasium, the Recreation Room, and other places, even including the Mall. And there are good people who surround you. If you come into contact with others who you feel are having a difficult time, I want to know that and I will meet with them. I repeat, all of this is an order. Fear is normal, but abdicating to fear leads to disaster both for people and for nations.

When the great Russian author, Aleksandr Solzhenitsyn was incarcerated by the Soviet Union, he was brought to a room in which he was told to sign his name to a confession of crimes he did not commit. He refused to sign. From an adjoining room he heard the screams of a woman. He was told someone he loved was in that room and he could end her torture by signing the document in front of him. He knew the screams could be coming from an actress or a tape. But he also knew the screams could be coming from someone he loved. He still refused to sign. In later years he was asked how he was able to continue to refuse signing the document under such conditions. He said—and I am paraphrasing—"I set my mind to believe that everyone I loved had gone on a train together, and the train crashed—a terrible accident—and they were all killed in that crash. It happens. Things like that happen. And so I thought, what did I have left in life? Ahhh, but there was one thing I had left in life and I knew it, and so I knew it must be retained. The one thing I had left in life was my honor."

I believe that most of your loved ones are safe. Many of you even had an opportunity to give them warning or they received warning from others. Most would not be harmed even without warning. Your thoughts must be on what you can do to insure that we win this war and that those you love in this generation and those who come after you in future generations will never have to go through the conditions under which fate and our duty have given us. You may well be the one person who can make the ultimate difference. As difficult as this may be to believe; one smile, one sparkle of your eyes, one reminder to others of your courage may well decide whether or not our nation lives on.

Acting President of the United States of America,
Eli Jared.

CHAPTER

6

Visitors

ACCORDING TO THE clock on the wall of Acting President Eli Jared's new and luxurious office, the sun of Tuesday, July 18 had already come up over the invisible Virginia horizon.

The sleepless night had been spent reading every emergency paper that was left for the position he now occupied, most papers written by those in bureaucracies of the Executive Branch of Government.

In the adjoining office which served as a reception room, sat Helen behind her desk. Throughout her adult life it almost became her name: Helen Behindherdesk. Helen was a somewhat overweight woman in her late fifties, maybe early sixties with brown curly hair. She had been assigned to be the assistant of Eli Jared and was living in fear: not only the natural fear of the war but the natural fear of Eli Jared. She did not quite understand that Eli Jared enjoyed being Eli Jared, particularly enjoyed being old and he wanted to be older, as though he wasn't old enough. He had learned to take advantage of age, knowing at this stage of his life and at this stage of his stature he could get away with teasing and scaring people by saying the most absurd things to them. They would rarely challenge him and he knew it. He was in no way presumptuous but he wanted to enjoy himself. Just as noticeable as his demeanor was that he was from the old-school of treating women with far more respect than he treated men. Since the 1960s this was a novelty. He always opened doors for women, gestured for them to go first, and unless it was an inappropriate occasion, he stood up for them, and pulled out chairs for them to sit or for them to rise. At the same time he would have no hesitancy to call them 'honey,' or 'gorgeous' or 'sweetheart' and generally even the most ardent women–liberationists not only accepted such words from him but were flattered by them. They had so recklessly abandoned femininity years-back that many had begun to doubt they had any, and he restored faith in themselves. With all his old-school behavior he knew and they knew that his words were meant to be compliments. None of this, however, was important to poor Helen Peterson who was scared to death of him out of fear she would do something wrong.

She emerged into the doorway of his office with her hands clasped in front of her in her usual posture of absolute decorum that made her look like a singer in a Verdi opera. "Ralph Ussery to see you, Mister President." Even such a simple sentence had been rehearsed when she had walked toward the doorway.

Eli Jared didn't call Helen 'honey' or 'gorgeous' or 'sweetheart.' He didn't even call her 'Helen.' He called her by her last name, 'Peterson.' "Good. Yes, good. Please ask him to come in, Peterson. Thank you." Acting President Jared moved his eye-patch from his left eye to the more informal position of having it rest against his forehead. He took off his reading glasses (one glass had long since been removed from the eye-glass frame) and put them on top of the stack of papers.

With some relief for apparently having done everything correctly, Helen turned her head to someone who was out of view from President Jared. "He'll see you now, Mr. Ussery."

President Jared left his desk and went to a lounge chair as Ralph Ussery, a balding man in his late forties in horn-rimmed glasses came in the office. Eli Jared respected Ralph Ussery as the head of Electronic and Digital Infrastructure, a craft of which little was known by Eli Jared who still had difficulty with anything that required an instruction book, and surely not an instruction CD.

"Sit down, Ussery. Sit down over here." He indicated for him to sit in the lounge chair opposite the one on which he was sitting. "You making any progress on communications?"

Ralph Ussery nodded. "Communications are, in many cases, restored."

"Oh, that's wonderful! Thank God! And thank you, Ussery!"

"Mister President, it's not that good. According to what I hear, and I don't know if it's true, but from what the revolutionaries are saying publicly, millions of Americans have been killed. The revolutionaries are in every big city in the United States. Or so they're saying. From the reports, our armed forces are losing everywhere—but I'm hearing this from the revolutionaries so I don't know if it's true. Television is telling nothing. It's just Islamic prayers and Imams and music; Mideast music, things like that. But on phones, on chatter, what they say is unthinkable. There is no confirmation. One of the reasons there is no confirmation or denial is that I'm very sorry to add, Mister President, something terribly important: there are holes in our communications. Big ones. To the best of my knowledge, no signal is getting out of here to the contingency locales or our military bases or to the designated codes for major Chiefs of State. It's like there's a shield around them. I think there is."

"Oh, my God! My heavens!"

"I'll keep trying, sir, but I've tried almost everything I can. I'll keep at it."

"My God! Are you talking about U.S. Strategic Command as well?"

"I am. That was the first place I attempted. And I've attempted to get hold of it repeatedly. Offutt Air Force Base where the Strategic Command is located is totally dead. No signals. Nothing. A total void."

"Oh, God!"

"Mister President, I have a belief about this, but only a belief."

"What?"

"I believe that they've used electromagnetic pulse weapons. I believe they had enough power to melt every piece of circuitry in communication devices here in Sebotus that connect us to our key contacts; our K.C.'s as we call the key contacts that are separate from the rest; or maybe they used electromagnetic pulse weapons to stop the sending of communications from our military bases, our contingency locations, and particular foreign locales. Either way, I think we are looking at electromagnetic pulse weapons. E.P.W.'s they're called. I don't know what perimeters they've penetrated but it could be they are around this facility or around all our K.C.'s. The best we can hope for is that it's only around ours."

"Can they do that, Ralph?"

"Yesterday, sir, I would have told you they couldn't do that. We have all kinds of 'cages' around our K.C. circuitry and so does everyone else have 'cages' around theirs. But today it appears to me as though it's been done."

"And no way to contact any of the Doomsday Planes?"

"Correct."

There was a long silence as Eli Jared got up and paced, then sat down again. "Keep at it, please. Keep at it, Ussery. Please, Ralph. And about the reports about millions killed—they can be false. I don't want anyone here to hear them. This place will be in panic. They have to keep their spirits. And those reports could be nothing but propaganda. What else do they say?"

"Justice being given to all infidels. And then all schools closed. They'll be opened for boys only. A lot of small things, too. Small in comparison. Strict clothing codes for everyone; things like that."

"No one can hear this, Ralph. Our spirits have to be maintained. All of this is rumor that can be designed for the purpose of destroying our determination. Remember that when it comes to *us,* they want to kill us if they know we're here. They can kill us just by spreading this kind of information. Do you understand what I mean, Ralph?"

"Yes, sir."

"Ralph—I want to see the reports. I want you to move the television monitor from this office to my apartment on the Succession Apartments Floor, and make sure it's connected to every commercial channel. I'll take that risk. Just make sure no other set with TV channels is operative."

"Yes, sir."

"And keep trying to get in contact with—with our people—our K.C.'s as you call them."

"I will, sir."

"Yes. Keep at it. A World War and it's on our own shores, and we can't find our President or our Strategic Command or—or anything. Thank you, Ussery. Thank you, Ralph. Tell Peterson I want to see her, will you please?"

"Who, sir?"

"Peterson. The girl out there. My secretary."

"Yes, sir."

After hearing from Helen Peterson, a select group of nine met in the Sebotus Situation Room (SSR). President Jared sat at the head of the table across from Admiral Kaylin. President Jared told them about the lack of communications with the contingency locales. He told them nothing about the other reports he heard. "I have issued an Executive Order and it is going out right now to everyone in Sebotus, staff and members alike, to turn in any electronic communications they may have independently. We cannot take the chance that our signals will be picked up by the revolutionaries. We don't know what technology the revolutionaries have and what they don't have. We know it's sophisticated enough to have knocked out all our communications with U.S. Strategic Command and all our contingency locales. I want you to see to it that there is not one sign of panic here. Not from you, not anyone else. Remain calm and get your bearings. Understood?

"Now, I have not called the entire cabinet together." And then with his usual immense command, he became more relaxed as though he was not burdened by events. "And you know why I didn't call the whole cabinet together here? Too many of them have no business being here. Frankly, I don't know what to do with them—not that any real president ever did. Every administration begins with the new president telling the country he will run a cabinet-oriented administration. It's bunk. In short time, cabinet officers become more loyal to their inherited bureaucracy than they do to the president. It takes a while but presidents learn. And to make matters worse, they soon find out that cabinet meetings are worthless. What are they going to talk about? They all have such diverse interests that they don't stick to the subject matter at hand or they don't know enough about it to make any intelligent comments. And those things of interest to some members are of no interest to others and too many of them are of no interest to the president. It's bunk.

"President Reagan used to fall asleep during cabinet meetings. That was to his credit. At least he got some sleep. Why on earth would President Kennedy have wanted to hear from his Postmaster General or from his Secretary of Health, Education, and Welfare during the Cuban Missile Crisis? So he didn't. So he created an ExCom as he called it; an Executive Committee. Just the people he wanted in it. And why, during Hurricane Katrina would President Bush want to hear from the Secretary of Veteran's Affairs? It's bunk. It's all bunk. So this is my ExCom. Maybe you could call it my National Security Council but I've excluded a couple of what would be the NSC members and included others whose jobs have never been included as part of it. Half the NSC's wouldn't have known what to do without a staff. So this is ExCom 2. You are all designated as members of ExCom 2. Nine of you and one of me. Now we are legal.

"Here's what we know. No. No. Here's what we don't know. I don't know if President Wadsworth is alive or dead. I don't know who is alive and dead outside of these walls. I don't know if our military is winning battles or losing them. We have to assume the worst of everything. Everything. All we have to do is concern ourselves with devising a plan—a plan to somehow . . . somehow bring about the enemy's defeat. You all have minds. Think like you have never thought before. We're not going to sit in Sebotus Headquarters coping. And I don't want plans on how we save our *own* necks. I want plans on how we save the *nation's* neck. We are going to do whatever must be done. So think. Think by yourselves. I want to have nine plans. Send them to me whenever you get done even if it takes you all night, but I want them on my desk by six o'clock tomorrow morning. We'll meet after I've studied them. Think like you have never thought before. Is that clear?"

"President Kennedy had thirty in his ExCom, sir," Acting Vice President and National Security Advisor Vernon Mapes said.

"I don't want historians, Vernon! I want thinkers."

And that's when a very loud alarm went off. President Jared assumed it was a test but it wasn't. Over the speaker system came the familiar feminine voice that seemed to make all announcements and who had no name and no face. "All eyes to the television monitors," she said and then repeated it. "All eyes to the television monitors."

And the television monitors exhibited surreal images. A helicopter had landed outside the Sebotus Headquarters. Seven men walked from the helicopter to the first door of the mountain. One of them put something in the slot outside the entrance. None of the barriers opened. And while the helicopter flew off spewing massive sprawls of dust around them, another of the men tried putting something in the slot but it accomplished nothing, while another attempted to engage a card into the DNA verification card-slot.

"That 'copter was not one of ours, sir," Vernon Mapes almost yelled.

"We can take care of this in very short time," President Jared said with amazing calm. "We don't even have to walk down the hall. We just happen to be in the right room at the right time. Do you know the protocol, Admiral?" President Jared asked Admiral Kaylin.

"I read it last night, Mister President. It was in the briefings they left for me."

President Jared gave a short nod. "That's when I read it. Did you put it to memory?"

"That was what my directive ordered. Yes, sir. It's in my memory and the card is with me."

"Do it. Let's hope it works. Do it, Admiral."

Admiral Kaylin gave a short, "Yes, Mr. President" and took a small card from his left breast pocket and moved to another chair. Then he "did it" with "it" meaning the insertion and drawback of the card into and out of a slot in the side of the table followed by pressing a yellow button that was inlaid into the table-top. That was followed by pressing a blue inlaid button next to the yellow one, and then a red inlaid button next to the blue one. He pressed the red one three short times and one longer one. Then he reinserted his card into the slot on the side of the table. Then President Jared pressed a button on his side of the table.

This procedure allowed the seven men outside headquarters to feel, if not see, a barrier open. The barrier was beneath their feet. It opened, swallowed them, and closed. It was close to being instantaneous giving no opportunity for its victims to move away.

"They've been swallowed, sir. It's done, Mr. President," Admiral Kaylin almost whispered.

President Jared closed his eyes for a few seconds, opened them and looked back at Admiral Kaylin. He nodded again and said, "Thank you, Admiral."

"Yes, sir."

None of the others said anything for maybe ten or fifteen seconds and whatever the span of time, it seemed like an hour. Vernon Mapes finally offered, "There will be more. They were either the first team sent to make an attempt or maybe a suicide squad to see what we could do. Maybe both."

President Jared shook his head slowly as he closed his eyes again, and then he put his elbows on the arms of the chair and formed a single fist with both hands. He rested his chin on top of the fist. "It doesn't make any difference who they were or what will be tried next—if anything. No one is going to get in. If more attempts are made, they'll just be killing themselves. Sebotus is beyond penetration. I hope they send an army. And then another army and another army. Because when the armies get close enough they'll be killed by us and all we have to do is lift a finger. If they send enough armies we'll win the war that way. And if they hold off sending armies and, instead, try to blast us out of here, they won't succeed that way either. This place can withstand a direct hit with a nuclear bomb."

Vernon Mapes at least appeared to be thinking deeply. "So what do you think they'll do, sir?"

"If they're smart, they'll do nothing. If they're brilliant they'll recognize that all they have to do is wait until we die. Sebotus can't prevent death by natural causes—like starvation."

There was no response.

"We can last four to six months. That's what they wrote in my briefing papers. We can last longer if I start rationing now."

Admiral Kaylin asked, "Are you going to order that?"

"No. There will be no rationing. We're not going to wait inside this place until we die. We aren't going to be in this place that long. We're only going to be in this place until we win. The worst thing we can do is start rationing and get everyone depressed thinking that this is the end and they have to spare the food to lengthen the time they can live. Let them *bathe* in the food. We're going to think our way into winning. Victory calls for optimism. Be concerned only with presenting to me your individual plans for victory. I told you, no more days of coping. Think. God gave you minds. This is why he gave you the minds you have. Now don't let anyone in this facility think of failure. After all, you have reason to be optimistic. We just killed seven enemy combatants, didn't we? There are seven less of them than there were just minutes ago."

* * *

Eli Jared went into the hall and coming the other way was Traci Howe, files under one arm and a few papers in her free hand. Eli Jared wanted to get out of the mood of what he had just been through and he knew exactly how to do it. He squinted his eyes as they came closer to each other in the hall. "What's your name again? Trudy? Tanya? Tammy? Trixie?" He knew her name.

She knew he knew. "Traci, Mister President. Traci Howe."

"Traci. Traci. That's right. I remembered. I remembered," he said so she would think he didn't remember. "Are you sure you aren't Joan of Arc?"

That wide smile with the perfect teeth. "I don't think so, Mister President."

"Well, I think you are. I think you're really Joan of Arc."

"You think? Why?"

"I hear good reports about you."

"From who?"

"From the press."

"From the press? What press?"

"Some newspaper. I don't remember which one."

"Mister President, you didn't learn anything from the press! There *is* no press here."

"I guess you're right. So what?"

"Mister President, do you always tease people?"

"Not always," and this time he smiled. "But it's fun. Life has to be fun. You can't let things get you down. Where do you work anyway? For Kaylin? Isn't that where I saw you?"

"Yes, sir. For Admiral Kaylin. I brought you to his office, remember?"

"That's right. That's right. Well, he's a good man. You're working for a good man. He's not as good looking as I am, naturally, but maybe he can have some plastic surgery done while he's here."

She laughed again. Then she raised her eyebrows in pretended seriousness. "I'll mention that to him."

"Tell him it's your idea. You take the credit."

"Oh, thank you. I will!" she teased back.

"Where you heading? To some silly beauty pageant? Miss America or something?"

"I don't think they have them here! Besides, I don't think I qualify. I'm going to the file room."

"I didn't know there was a file room. There's a room for every thing imaginable in this place."

"Maybe, but you or someone else might want some document quickly. It's important to have a file room where everything is cross-indexed every possible way. I established the indexing system here months ago. It was my job here before—before all this happened."

"Alright, alright, alright. I take it back; you're not Joan of Arc."

"I'm not? Why not?"

"I minimized you that way. That's what. I think if Joan of Arc was told she was somewhat like you, now that would have been more like it. That would have been a compliment for the old dame."

Traci laughed. "Thank you. But I really don't mind being compared to Joan of Arc."

"Well, have a safe trip to the file room. There's a lot of strange people in these halls. Be careful."

"Oh, I will be, Mister President."

They both walked in opposite directions but he turned his head to take one more look at her as she walked away. He mumbled to himself, "Make a preacher lay his Bible down."

Eli Jared went back to the opulence of the Presidential Office and sat at his glass-topped desk. At another time he would have raptured in the luxury. Not now. Reality came back and luxury was a poor substitute for the security of the nation. What he had not told the others in the Situation Room was that he already had a plan. And the plan would be exercised unless one of them came up with something of greater ingenuity and promise.

Without punching the button on his interoffice communication box he simply yelled, "Peterson?"

It was only a few seconds before she appeared at the doorway, her frightened eyes taking up half the room on her face. "Yes, Mister President?"

"I want you to get Wayne Stuart over here."

She looked confused. "Who, sir?" she asked cautiously.

"Wayne Stuart."

"Is he with Sebotus, sir?" and her hands went to their more normal interlock in front of her.

"Sebotus *staff.* He's on *staff.*"

"Yes, sir," she said and disappeared to once again become her normal Helen Behindherdesk.

Only one minute passed before Eli Jared buzzed the interoffice communication box.

"Yes, Mister President," Helen Peterson answered the buzz.

"Where is he? Where's Wayne Stuart? What's up?"

With some breathlessness she said, "I'm on the line, sir, trying to get him. There's been no answer."

"What do you mean there's been no answer?"

"He might be in the men's room. Maybe that's where he is."

"Get him out of there, Peterson. I want to see him."

"Yes, sir. I'll do my best."

"Not good enough! Do better than your best."

Two minutes later there was a buzz on his interoffice communication box.

"Yes, Peterson?"

"Mr. President, Secretary Glass would like to see you."

"Who's that? Who's Secretary Glass? Where's Wayne Stuart?"

Now she talked fast in an attempt to get it all out quickly. "I'm still having difficulty getting him, sir. In the meantime the Secretary of HUD, Angus Glass is here. He said it's important."

"Oh, God; Angus Glass! What does he want? Wait. Wait. Is he standing right there in your office?"

"Yes, sir."

"Can he hear me or do you have earphones on?"

"Yes, sir."

"Yes, sir, what? Okay, you can't answer which one. I get it, Peterson. Just say yes or no. Can he hear me?"

"No, sir."

"Do you have earphones on?"

"Yes, sir."

"Good. Listen, tell him—oh, God, let me see. Tell him that I have my hands full but he can have three or four minutes—and that's it: three minutes or four minutes and then tell him I have to go to a briefing. Got it, Peterson?"

"Yes, sir. I will, sir."

"Time him. And in three minutes get him out of here. And if you get Wayne Stuart before then, tell Stuart to get himself over here, and I'll get rid of Glass myself. Got it, Peterson?"

"Yes, sir."

Angus Glass walked in and gave a quick look around the office he had never seen before. "This is nice, sir." He sat down opposite Eli Jared who was still sitting behind his desk. "Sir, the reason for my visit may not be any of my business but—"

"You're Secretary of Housing and Urban Development, aren't you, Angus?"

"Yes, sir."

"If you want to build some houses or demolish some shopping malls, then it is your business. Just tell me what you want to destroy or build and I'll give it consideration that would be due the Secretary of Housing and Urban Development."

Without showing any intimidation, Angus Glass answered, "I'm in the line of succession, sir, so I would think I should have a voice in some of the policies carried out here, sir."

"You bet you do. Shoot."

"What, sir?"

"Shoot. Shoot. Shoot. What's your advice?"

"Was the Attorney General consulted before you buried those seven men alive, sir?"

"Of course not."

"Of course not?"

"Didn't you hear me, boy? I said 'of course not.'"

"Yes, sir. I heard you. Sir, there has to be some kind of judicial review before we kill people."

Eli Jared stared at Angus Glass for a while before he said very softly, "I see." Another pause. "I see." Another pause. "That's your advice, Mr. Acting Secretary?"

"Yes, sir, because we can't be as uncaring about life as our opponents. What good is giving up everything the Founders wanted us to be and start using the same tactics as our opponents?"

Again, "I see. Yes, yes, the Founders."

"Yes, sir."

"Mr. Acting Secretary—Mr. Glass—the Founders would have long ago put you in shackles."

Angus Glass hesitated and then asked, "For what offense, sir?"

"Ignorance. Stupidity."

Now Angus Glass was, of course, insulted. "The Founders didn't make such judgments, sir."

"How the devil do you know?"

"I'm an historian, sir. I took U.S. history at U.C.L.A. and I received top honors."

"What did you do? Get an 'A'?"

"Yes, sir."

"My, God, an 'A' student! I didn't know I had an 'A' student here in this facility. What good fortune!"

"Yes, sir."

"You see, I didn't do very well in school. Mrs. Bendel was my home room teacher in junior high and she told me I wasn't paying attention. It was rough for me in school. I was looking at the girls. That's all I did. You know how that is, Glass."

"Uh-huh."

"My boy, tell me a little about your experiences after you got out of school."

"Well, sir, after I got my Masters; my MBA, I took a Civil Service Exam, and I passed quite well in comparison with the others. And then within weeks I got a job as a GS-12 right away in the Department of Education, and then was transferred to Housing and Urban Development and in the years since then I kept advancing all the way to an Assistant Secretary. And now, as you know, all the way to Acting Secretary of HUD."

President Jared nodded as he looked deep in thought. "That's impressive. Very impressive. I'll tell you what. I'll give thought to what you just advised, but assuming I take your advice, I want to know what you would do right now if you were me. What do you think I should do?"

"What do you mean, sir?"

"We're at war, you know."

"Yes, I know."

"How do I win?"

"How do you win?"

"I want to win. How do I do that? What's your plan? If it's a good plan I want to use it."

"We win honorably, sir."

"Good. Good. I like that. Honorably. Yes. Win honorably. Anything else? I mean that's a pretty short plan."

"Fair trials."

"Check!" President Jared thumped the desk with his fist.

"Fair trials even for the worst of them."

"Check!" President Jared thumped the desk with his fist again.

"With attorneys."

"Check!" And another thump. "We have plenty of attorneys in the cabinet."

"Always by the rules of the Geneva Conventions."

"Check! Check!" Again, the thump this time followed by a second thump. "Of course, the Geneva Conventions."

That's when the buzzer went off on his intercom, and Helen's voice told him, "Mr. President, it's time for your briefing. You are running late."

"Give me another minute, Peterson. Tell them I'll be right there." He snapped the intercom off. "Now, Angus, I have to hurry along. By the Geneva Conventions, hey? Good advice, Glass. I'll consider that. I want to give some thought to the well thought-out advice you gave me. Let me think."

It was quiet for a half-minute while Eli Jared thought as he put his hand on his chin and looked down. Then, after the half-minute was done he jolted his face up to look directly in Angus Glass's eyes and he broke the silence by saying, "I thought about it."

"Will you do it, sir?"

"Do what?"

"Live by the rules of the Geneva Conventions."

"I go back further than that. I go back to the Founders, just like you said at first. I liked that. And I told you they would have put you in shackles for your stupidity, didn't I? Something like that."

"That's what you said, sir, but I don't think you meant it."

"Well, I suppose I wouldn't really know exactly what they did, of course. I told you about home room teacher in junior high . *You* would know. You're an historian, aren't you?"

"Yes, sir."

"Then I'm sure you remember what I *did* study: When the Revolutionary War was fought, we were ruthless. I mean ruthless. It was the only way we could win. Now the situation is even worse than what was faced by the Founders so I will go further than just being ruthless. Tonight, as Acting President of the United States I have determined that during this time of emergency, stupidity is a capital offense. I will call in the firing squad."

Angus Glass knew that Eli Jared was not serious but he also knew that his credentials did not impress his audience of one. Nor did his answers to the questions posed by Eli Jared raise his prestige. He regretted that his advice to the Commander in Chief would never be taken seriously, even though he was giving his advice as Acting Secretary of Housing and Urban Development.

CHAPTER

7

The Solarium

IT WASN'T REALLY outside, but the view through the floor-to-ceiling 360-degree window was such a magnificent simulation of the outside that it was nearly impossible to tell it was the creation of Man six years ago and not created by God six million years ago. The leaves of the oak trees moved, each oak tree giving a small sway of its own separate from one another with any gust of wind that came from some out-of-view source. And the sky was blue at times and gray at times and there was sunrise and sunset at the appropriate hours and there was often rain and if it was winter there were days and nights of snow. It was the idea of a creative mastermind with considerable artistry who directed a team of talented disciples who faithfully copied every detail of the Shenandoah Valley as seen from Virginia's Skyline Drive. The giant room with the treasured window was called the Solarium of the Sebotus.

There were those who had argued against the construction of the

Solarium but they lost to its inventor, Wayne Stuart of the Sebotus staff, who was visionary enough to believe there could come the time when it might be needed, and genius enough to create it.

Admiral Kaylin sat there alone. He sat on one of the four brown leather chairs facing the night with a full moon shining on a distant waterfall through the west view of the window. His assignment for the evening was to think; that most difficult assignment having been commissioned by the President. On his lap was a yellow legal pad with many pages having been filled with the completed pages rolled back behind the top spine of the pad. He stared at the clean yellow sheet facing him and then, inspired from memory, he scrawled a quote of William Shakespeare: "Cowards die many times before their deaths. The valiant never taste of death but once."

The intercom gave the familiar signal of dot-dot-dot-dash in the pattern of the first four notes of Beethoven's Fifth Symphony.

"Yes, sir?" he said.

But it wasn't a sir. It was Traci Howe. "Admiral Kaylin? It's Traci."

"Oh, I'm sorry. Yes, ma'am. Yes, Traci."

"I'm going to my residence. Is there anything you need before I go down? I'm not planning on coming back to the office this evening unless you need something."

"No, no. I'm fine. Thank you, Traci."

"You sure? I'm going to the cafeteria first, Admiral. Can I pick up some food for you? I don't think you had lunch. Did you miss dinner too, sir?"

He gave a short laugh. "I missed it. You're right. I'll go there later and get something. But thank you, Traci."

"You sure? I can pick up a Big Mac."

"Do you they have Big Macs?"

"Not real ones but they look like them and they're good."

"You're getting to know me pretty well," and he gave another short laugh.

"Want one?"

He thought for a while. "No, I want two."

"Really?"

"That does sound good."

"And french fries?"

"Oh, that—that does sound good."

"Anything else?"

"No. No. I wasn't hungry at all before you started mentioning the Big Mac. I wasn't even thinking of food. That was before you started this. Yes. I want two Big Macs or whatever they are, and I want french fries, a thing of salt, those things they have. And I want coffee with some cream, and I want a doughnut with orange frosting—if they have one."

"Good! Alright. I'll do it. What if they don't have orange frosting?"

"Anything. Then just a plain cake-doughnut. Not the glazed kind. And please get yourself anything you want. I'm taking you. I don't mean I'm taking you there, but please—please bring your food up here with mine. Tell them I'm buying. Sign my name or whatever you have to do there."

Traci's voice had a smile. "Is that an invitation?"

"You bet."

There was an even greater smile in her voice. "That's the worst invitation I have ever had in my life. Boy, if that wasn't a second thought!"

He didn't laugh out loud but almost. "I'm sorry. It did sound that way. I didn't mean it that way."

"Oh, I know. Admiral, they don't charge anything here. There is nothing to buy. Neither one of us can pay."

"Oh, that's right. I forgot."

"Admiral, I think you have other things on your mind."

"The only thing I have on my mind now is that I'm hungry. It's past dinner-time and I didn't even have lunch. I didn't, did I?"

Since she had already told him he didn't have lunch, she didn't think his question was worthy of an answer. "Admiral, where do I go after the cafeteria to get to you? Where is the Solarium?"

"It's the 6A button of the elevator. When you get to the door set your pass to 71, wait a couple seconds, then press 883. Don't write it down. Can you remember it?"

"Don't write it down?"

"That's for sure. Don't even repeat it. Do you know the numbers I gave you? 71, wait two or three seconds, then press 883."

"I remember. If I make a mistake I'll knock."

While waiting for Traci and all the food he requested, he re-read the material he had written on the yellow legal pad including the Shakespeare line that concluded his writing. He carefully tore the pages from the pad and put them in an envelope and marked the envelope "Eyes Only: President Eli Jared." He sealed the envelope and set it down on the table in front of the lounge chairs. He heard the clicking of someone's pass, and then the door opened.

Traci Howe stood there in absolute awe. The door closed by itself behind her and she didn't move. The surprising spectacle of the view from the Solarium was described best by the only word that came to her mind: "Heaven!" To see what looked like the outside was more welcome than any view she could have imagined she would see from Sebotus. She continued to stand motionless holding two large filled bags. "This is heaven!"

Admiral Kaylin nodded. "Yes, it is."

"Oh! I can't believe it!" She took in the entire expanse, now even turning behind her where only the door interrupted the glass enclosure. "How come there's a window? I thought there were no windows anywhere here."

"There aren't. I suppose technically it's a window, but it doesn't separate this room from the outside. All of that in front of you—behind the glass—is inside. Please come in further."

She shook her head. "Not yet. I want to look."

"Alright. Then after you get done standing, you can go right up to it and look at it closer—and give me those Big Macs."

"I never knew the outside is heaven, Admiral."

"It always has been. But it isn't thought of that way until you can't reach it."

She came in further, opened the bags and handed him the cheeseburgers, putting the other items he wanted on one of the chairs next to him, and she sat on the other side of him with her dinner on her lap.

The food was no more. He had eaten all she brought back for him. She had eaten a salad, and they both had coffee accompanied by orange-frosted doughnuts and he was on a second cup of coffee, that second cup thoughtfully provided by Traci without his request, and he had that second cup accompanied by a cigarette.

They sat side by side on those two of the four leather chairs facing the west view.

"Thank you, Traci, for getting dinner."

"Oh, I thank you for allowing me to see this—this miracle."

"It is miraculous. I'll stay here for just a little while longer. I still have a little more to do."

"Aren't you going to go to your residence now, Admiral?"

"No. Not for a while. Not only do I have more to do but I've seen enough of the residence. Besides, I can't sleep well and I want to be tired when I go there."

"Ever since all this started I haven't slept well, either. I don't think anyone does."

He nodded. "Our minds are too filled with thoughts. And fears. I don't know if anyone in the nation can sleep these nights. Everyone in the nation is frightened."

"Not the terrorists." She remembered the staff's Code of Conduct.

"You're right. Not the terrorists. They're celebrating."

For a while there was no conversation.

Then Traci said his name as a question, "Admiral Kaylin?"

"Yes?"

She hesitated before putting her question into words, and even though she remembered the Code of Conduct, she asked, "We are very close to death, aren't we?" It was a question, she reasoned, and not a statement, and she wanted to know his answer.

He stared directly in her eyes. He hesitated and then answered. "Traci, that might be."

She nodded slowly. "Does 'might be' mean 'probably are'?"

He shook his head. "Traci, do you believe in God?"

She answered with no hesitation. "I do."

"You're that sure?"

"Why? You don't?"

"It isn't that. I'm simply honest enough to tell you I don't know. I've been trying to figure it out throughout my life. Have you ever thought that maybe you believe in God because you *want* to believe in God?

"I believe in God because there isn't anything logical that gives me another choice."

"Isn't evolution logical?"

"Yes. Totally. I believe in evolution. I believe in both."

"Really? That's a new one. Isn't it one or the other? I don't know which. Right now there's the threat of death and I don't kid myself about it—or kid you about it. And I do want to believe in God but I don't know if I do. Everyone tells me I just have to have faith. I don't know if faith is good enough for me."

"I didn't mention faith."

"But you're going to mention faith, aren't you?"

"I'm going to mention movies."

He looked at her with a struggled look on his face as he shook his head. Visually he was asking, "What are you talking about?" Audibly he was mute, unable to think of anything to say.

"Admiral, I wanted to be a movie star."

He felt like saying "So what?" but he said, "You did?"

"Yes. First, I wanted to be a model but I was too short. No one took me seriously. That's when I decided I wanted to be a movie star. I sang. I always sang. And I danced. I was even in two Off-Broadway shows. I got good reviews, too. Bob Button wrote, 'Watch this girl. Remember her name. You'll hear it again and again. Traci Howe is Traci And How!' I memorized that line. So I took it seriously and I knew in order to be a movie star I needed to know everything I could about movies. Not just musicals. I thought maybe I could be a movie star when I was young but even if I made it, some day I would be old and then I would be a director or a producer or something and I wanted to know everything there was to know about movies. That's how I found out more about religion than I did about movies."

"What do you mean?"

And she broke out in more than he anticipated, signaling he was not going to get out of there quickly. "Movies started with Edison; Tom Edison thinking of a device he called the kinetoscope. It was a little cabinet. People looked in it through a hole and saw what appeared to be all kinds of images moving inside. Pictures. It was a strand of still pictures shown through a shutter so you couldn't see the strand moving but saw each picture standing still and, very quickly, each still picture moved to the next one. The illusion was that horses inside the cabinet were racing each other. Like a flip-book. As time went on, pictures like that were projected on a white wall and a man flicked at sixteen pictures a second as he sneezed, over and over again. Then fire engines raced from the left of the white wall to the right of the white wall. Then the walls were built in a cheap fabric that provided a screen wherever they could be hung. Then a film was shot of a pretty woman tied to a railroad track by a villain with a big mustache and he twirled the mustache and audiences booed and hissed him. Then in the theaters that displayed these pictures, an organ player was hired to play music next to the screen and he created a mood with the music. Then the images were shot with better lenses and the softness became sharp and then the pictures were shot and projected at twenty-four pictures a second rather than sixteen and the motion was a lot smoother. Then on the screen, a man knelt and sang and the audience was amazed because they not only could see him move his mouth but they could hear him sing! Then the images changed from black-and-white to color. Then came Walt Disney's '*Fantasia*' with Fantasound with multi-speakers in the theater. And that evolved into stereophonic sound. Then the screens became huge. Admiral Kaylin, the motion picture evolved. But each step of the evolution was created by someone. None of the steps just appeared by themselves. You agree?"

Admiral Kaylin was transfixed. This pretty little 'Girl Friday' was more than what she appeared to be, and more than he would ever have known if he hadn't asked her about believing in God. "I'm impressed. You're quite something."

"Do you agree with me? Do you agree?"

He nodded. "I have to think about it. What you say makes sense but what I can't quite handle is that if there is a God, then would He create what we see today: Terrorists? People who are so horrible. If God exists, why would he create them?"

"Because—because through that whole thing I just gave you about movies, through that whole evolution, there were good movies and there were bad movies. Terrible ones. None of the creators wanted to create flops. They wanted to create good movies. Something like creating life, isn't it? That doesn't mean there wasn't a Creator. Creators made movies and some of them turned out good and some of them turned out bad. So don't blame God."

Then Admiral Kaylin noticed that her nose was running. He reached in his back pocket and pulled out a white handkerchief. With a smile, he leaned to her and wiped the handkerchief below her nose.

"It's running again?"

He smiled and nodded.

"It always runs. I have allergies, I think."

He gave another nod and put the handkerchief back in his pocket. "Traci?"

"Yes."

"Do you believe in Heaven and Hell?"

She thought for a while, and then shook her head. "I wish I knew. I don't know. I asked God that question once if there was Heaven and Hell. I think that's when he gave me the allergies. So I don't ask Him anymore."

Admiral Kaylin laughed. "I don't think so, Traci."

"I don't blame Him for giving me the allergies. I was too curious so he got me in the nose. It was in the same conversation when I asked Him if He lived in Empyrean."

"Where?"

"Empyrean."

"What's that?"

"You don't know? Oh, Admiral, there's a place called Empyrean. In school I was told that the ancient Greeks said it was the highest heaven. The heaven above heaven."

"Really?"

"That's what they said. I was always fascinated by it. Can you imagine? A heaven above heaven. He didn't answer me when I asked Him, but can you imagine a heaven above heaven? That must really be something. "

"That's where you're going, Traci."

She gave him a silent look. And he stared at her. Then she turned her face back to the window and squinted at the view. "Is it raining? Look! There's rain."

"A little. Not heavy."

"But it's raining!"

"It is."

"And there's wind. Those trees over there—the thin ones are swaying. See the leaves? They're blowing."

"Yes, they are."

"Don't you wish we could go out there? And walk in the rain?"

He gave his short smile, and he nodded. "But it isn't outside, and we can't get outside. And not to—what we're looking at. I'm grateful just to have the view."

"Oh, me too. I am, too."

And because neither of them wanted to turn the conversation back to matters of theology, they stared at the trees and the rain and the breeze and the black sky with its moon, and the light it shed on all those things.

He looked over at her. "Don't you want to go to your residence, Traci? It's late. It's close to midnight."

She looked at him sharply, almost as if she was angry. "I want to see sunrise."

He didn't look back at the view of the simulation of outside through the glass. Traci was the view. And she was not a simulation. They both looked at each other without a word. And then he said, "Sunrise won't be until hours from now. Not for six or so hours."

"You think?"

He gave her a slight, unavoidable smile. "I think."

Her eyebrows went up almost into the area of her face normally reserved for her forehead. "I want to see the sunrise!" It was either a plea or an order, depending on how it was to be interpreted. "You don't have to stay here, Admiral. Can't I stay here?" In a quick moment she had returned not only to being a young woman; but she returned to being a girl.

"You aren't cleared to be here alone, Traci. Those are the rules. I would like to let you stay here alone, but I can't do that."

"Then stay here with me. Can't I stay here, Admiral, to see sunrise?"

"Traci, I told you that won't happen for about six hours."

"Can't I stay for it?"

She did.

So did Admiral Kaylin.

And he was right. It took about six hours.

CHAPTER

8

After Sunrise

AFTER WEDNESDAY MORNING'S sunrise it was not long before the room turned bright but its brightness isn't what woke them. It was that invisible woman's voice on the speaker blaring, "All designated members of Acting President Jared's ExCom 2 please report to the Solarium at eight a.m. All designated members of Acting President Jared's ExCom 2 please report to the Solarium at eight a.m."

They both jolted as soon as the word "Solarium" was said for the first time. Then they stared into the other's face, no more than inches apart. Admiral Kaylin quickly looked at his wrist watch then took his arm from around Traci. Traci gave a contented smile and closed her eyes again, but not Admiral Kaylin. He jumped up and quickly assembled himself.

"Can't we stay for a while?" She was not in any hurry at all.

"Traci. It's seven-thirty. Do you want the whole committee to come here and see us? And President Jared?"

"How much time does that give us?"

"No time at all. They'll be here in less than a half hour. I have to get cleaned up quick; I have to straighten this place up, and you have to vamoose."

"Do you *want* me to go?" Only a woman.

"No. No. I don't *want* you to go, but you *have* to go."

"You think?"

"I know!"

It came to be that *she* straightened up the place before leaving since most of the clutter was due to her clothes being scattered all over the floor. Admiral Kaylin unashamedly gave her the empty cafeteria bags to take out with her, then began the torture of competing with the hands of his watch as he went about the hurried tasks of cleaning himself up, shaving, and looking somewhat respectable as anyone would want to look should the world be scheduled to end in short time with other people around.

Then he saw it. On the table in front of the lounge chairs was the envelope he marked "Eyes Only: President Eli Jared." It was now five minutes before eight o'clock and he had failed to deliver it. Too late. Two members of ExCom 2 came in the Solarium. Admiral Kaylin had to act as though he came in minutes before them. They looked so respectable.

They were followed by the entrance of Eli Jared. The two members who preceded him looked at the view through the window with expressions of amazement.

"Admiral?" Eli Jared said which meant "hello."

"Mister President," Admiral Kaylin responded in the appropriate way of answering the short greeting.

And then Eli Jared started sniffing, and then he started pacing while he was sniffing. He walked around the room. Then he looked at Admiral Kaylin. Neither one said anything until Eli Jared said, very softly, "I didn't get your advice, Admiral."

"Oh, I know, sir. I have it right here. I brought it with me. It took a little longer to write than I hoped," and he handed him the envelope.

Eli Jared grunted and looked at the envelope in his hand. "It says 'Eyes Only.' It should say 'Eye Only.' You know, I only have one of them." He pointed to his right eye. Then he pointed to his left eye. "You probably never noticed but I have a patch." Then he felt around the area of his face near the top left of his nose, but, of course, the patch wasn't over his left eye; it was on his forehead. He quickly pulled it down to cover his left eye. "See? I have a patch. Blind. The eye is blind."

Admiral Kaylin smiled. "I know, sir."

Then the door opened and other members of ExCom 2 came in. They walked all around the room, looking at the surprising view of a rainy day in Virginia's mountains in what appeared to be the outside. They murmured among themselves about the view, thinking the view was really the outside. Then a stranger came in; a young man of medium height with black hair and thin-rimmed glasses, dressed in a dark blue sports jacket and gray slacks. His face and manner had a unique look of depth that perceptive people could recognize in an instant. It was as though he was thinking of things they weren't thinking.

Eli Jared looked at the guests and nodded. "Sit down! Sit down! Sit down! Sit down! I read all your reports or whatever they are. Your advice. I read all of them except Kaylin's here. I just got Kaylin's. He was late. He just gave it to me. Let me read Kaylin's advice. Then we'll talk." It was the first time Admiral Kaylin heard Eli Jared say his name without the preface of 'Admiral.' Eli Jared plopped down on the same lounge chair that had been taken by Traci Howe. No one was sitting next to him. "It seems Kaylin had other things to do rather than get the paper in to me on time."

For the first time Admiral Kaylin became a target. All his colleagues looked at him or at least glanced at him. If Eli Jared showed disapproval, they would show disapproval.

Eli Jared looked at the young stranger. "Wayne—come here, boy." He patted the chair next to him where Admiral Kaylin sat last night with Traci Howe. Wayne Stuart sat there while Eli Jared tore open the envelope given to him previously by Admiral Kaylin. Then he unfolded the yellow legal-sized papers from the envelope. Everyone was quiet as he read the papers by holding them only inches away from his right eye. Then he tossed them down on the floor. "What the devil is this about, Kaylin?"

"What do you mean, sir?"

"What you wrote on the last page. Here. Here. Wait." And he leaned down, picked up the pages and found the last one and put it near his right eye. "'Cowards die many times before their deaths. The valiant never taste of death but once.'"

"That's Shakespeare, sir. I wanted to wrap it up that way. It summarized what I had written."

"Shakespeare! Very Harvard of you."

"I didn't go to Harvard, sir. I went to Annapolis."

"Good! That's good! But I'm not going to take your advice." Some of the others looked a little smug until Eli Jared added, "And I'm not going to take any of the advice that any of you wrote. Do you know why? Because all you showed was your willingness to die and I don't think you have much choice, judging from your advice. It's very noble to say we have to die in one way or another and that's all we can do. This may surprise you but I have no interest in volunteering death. Not yours, not mine, not one American's. I wanted creative ideas, not papers on the value of martyrdom. If we have to die to win, that's one thing. That's worth it. But no one is suggesting winning. There isn't one idea here about how to win. They're all ideas on how to die. It's how to lose with our boots on. I don't care if we die with our boots on or are barefoot. Let's win this thing."

There was silence and there were some nods.

"But thank God one person has a solution. One person is creative enough to have thought this through before it ever happened. Gentlemen, I want you to meet Wayne Stuart. He isn't a member of Sebotus. He's on the Sebotus staff. He met with me last night and we talked until early morning while you were all sleeping. I invited him here this morning. Gentlemen, take a look through the windows that surround us here. What you are looking at is an illusion created by Wayne Stuart. You're not looking at the outside. You're not even looking at a third-dimensional image. It's flat. It is all a fake. A fake. A magnificent fraud."

There were looks and even sounds of astounded reaction. Among those present, only President Jared, Admiral Kaylin, and, of course, Wayne Stuart had ever been in the Solarium before. "Those are no more the mountains of Virginia than I am. And that is no more rain in the Shenandoah Valley than it is—than it is—I don't know—than it is sand in . . . sand in the Sahara Desert. It is the work of an artist whose paints and brushes are mixed with imagination, photography, skill, and computers. Mr. Stuart. It all comes out of the mind of Mr. Stuart. This view has been here for six years. When it was completed, President Wadsworth invited me up here to see this room and to see what Wayne Stuart had created. I was absolutely dazzled. After I left here that day I thought about what Mr. Stuart had created and I thought about what he might do next, based on what he already did here—and based on my experiences with General Daniel Graham and Buzz Aldrin many years ago—the end of the 1970s when Dan Graham came up with his idea of High Frontier utilizing some 432 satellites. It wasn't for something like this—it was for a missile defense system but some of the elements of his idea seemed to me they could be applicable here. Graham's idea gave birth to Reagan's program for his Strategic Defense Initiative. So after I saw what Mr. Stuart did here, that memory of Graham kept rattling around in my head and about a week later—maybe a couple days more—I asked him to come to the White House to the office that President Wadsworth was kind enough to let me use when an occasion arose. I told Mr. Stuart I had a far-fetched idea for him to consider. At least it was far-fetched at the time. But I knew I was talking to a creative genius, so 'far-fetched' wouldn't mean anything to him. He said he would work on it. He was excited," and he looked at Wayne Stuart. "Weren't you?"

"Yes, sir."

Eli Jared looked back at the others. "I expressed to him this thought: Since 9-11 we have lived at a time when there has been a surrealistic superimposure of the dark ages and space-age technology. They live together. Islamist terrorists video-taped beheadings to exhibit around the world; we read text messages on a Blackberry regarding a missile attack on Haifa; cell-phones were used to detonate explosives; terrorists used internet websites for indoctrination; in the comfort of our living rooms we watched satellite transmissions of combat as it took place; and periodically we heard newly released audio tapes of the victims of attacks. Let's let technology work for us and not for them. Not for what they want *us* to see and hear, but what we want *them* to see and hear.

"In foreign policy there are times for everything. There are times for diplomacy, times for economic threats, times for military engagements, times for covert actions, and times for artistry. And so you have the State Department for diplomacy, the Commerce Department for economic threats, the Pentagon for military engagements, and the CIA for covert actions. There's nothing for artistry. And so we created it. Not we, but Mr. Stuart did. As for me, all I did was give the nod and say 'go ahead, Mr. Stuart.'

"You'll hear the idea in a second. We both knew that people in the bureaucracy and in the congress would say we were crazy. We, therefore, knew the importance of keeping it secret and we did exactly that. If one other person knew, it would no longer be a secret—not in this town. Maybe not in any town. And so Mr. Stuart couldn't tell anyone; not even the people he worked for here at Sebotus Headquarters.

"I told him that once before the United States used technology to its fullest in a grand piece of inventiveness. In 1961 President Kennedy said that this nation should commit itself to achieving the goal, before the decade was out, of landing a man on the moon and returning him safely to earth. At the time it was so crazy—so outrageous. No one knew how it could be done. At that time, in fact just twenty days earlier our largest accomplishment in space was nothing more than sending a man, Alan Shepherd, up into space and back down again—not even in orbit. He went up and down. No more. And the Mercury space capsule he was in fit him like a suit. No room for anything. But President Kennedy not only had the guts to initiate a lunar mission, but he set a deadline on that imaginative and untried idea. He had the help of the greatest rocket scientist of the time—Werner von Braun. And so the deadline was set to go to the moon before the decade was out.

"To do it, for the first time in history, inventions were scheduled—scheduled to achieve his goal. All of that because President Kennedy said 'do it!' They had to invent one thing by March of 1962, something else by December of '62, another invention by August of 1963, something else by some date in 1964, '65, '66, '67, '68, '69—before the clocks turn to 1970. And it was done. The goal was achieved in 1969 with Apollo 11. Before the decade was out man was on the moon and returned safely to the earth. Artistry. Creativity. Far-fetched. The impossible was done. Buck Rogers, Jules Verne, and H. G. Wells had become Neil Armstrong, Buzz Aldrin, and Michael Collins.

"Now let me take you to when Mr. Stuart finished what you're looking at here in the Solarium. There was something to do before *this* decade was out. And Wayne Stuart would have to be the inventor—the Werner von Braun of our time. And with no position of authority at all I had to copy President Kennedy by simply saying —do it.

"I promised him," and he looked over again at Wayne Stuart, "that I would stay out of your hair. And I did stay out of your hair, didn't I?"

"Yes, sir."

Eli Jared looked away from him to rescan the others. "You know why I stayed out of his hair? Something I learned when I was just a boy. I learned it in high school from an art teacher; Mr. Pratt, who was telling the class how important it is to leave creative people alone and not to bother them. Now I'm not one to quote historical figures. I leave that up to Admiral Harvard here to do that," and he took a quick glance at Admiral Kaylin. "But Mr. Pratt told us that when Diogenes was visited by Alexander the Great, Alexander asked him if he could do anything for him. Mr. Pratt said that Diogenes is quoted as answering Alexander by saying, 'Only stand out of my light.'

"Now, I'm the first to admit I'm no Alexander but the lesson was learned. So I left Mr. Stuart alone. And he did it. No permission, no authority, no conversation, but he took it on his own to go on to what we discussed. He recorded his costs to the Sebotus Accounting Office as 'miscellaneous' and sometimes to 'computer repair' or what other categories did you use?" Eli Jared looked back at Wayne Stuart.

Wayne Stuart answered, "I used 'canvas supplies' and 'hard disk upgrades' and 'scanning operations' and 'Microsoft coordination.' I guess they were things that wouldn't be understood but wouldn't be questioned."

"You mean you made up things with terms that would escape the notice of your superiors, right?"

"That's right. And I used a lot of initials that had no meaning. R.D.L.'s and F.F.P.'s. People in government hate to admit they don't know what something means. Particularly initials or acronyms."

Then Eli Jared looked away from Wayne Stuart and gave quick glances to each of the others. "He lied. He knew no one would approve what he was doing, such wild thinking that he was working on. Insubordination? Absolutely. He's an insubordinate who chose insubordination over the death of the nation. God love him." Then he looked back at Wayne Stuart. "Mr. Stuart, tell all of us what you've accomplished, boy." Then he again scanned the group of men. "We'll find out if we execute him for defrauding the Sebotus Accounting Department or if we give him the Medal of Freedom."

Wayne Stuart took the floor like a professional. He was so sure of his subject that he had no reason to be uneasy, no matter the significance of his audience. "It's not what I accomplished. If it wasn't for that idea of Mr. Jared after he saw what we had already done, and if it wasn't for a great team of those who worked on it without any of my team ever questioning what it was for, it wouldn't have been done. The team I put together had already been cleared by Sebotus Security for other things—they had worked with me on this room and the view that surrounds us now.

"To understand the proposal, take a look at that view. That's what

I invited Mr. Jared to see six years ago. Right after that is when he presented his idea to me. Let me first explain the view here as you can see it. Just like you can see rain right now and you can see every tree swaying separate and apart from the others, I can cast any other images in superimposure. I can cast the image of hundreds, even thousands of soldiers coming forward from the horizon with weapons that appear to be firing. I can fill the sky with combat aircraft. I can have missile nosecones appear to enter the atmosphere and come down on earth all the way to produce mushroom clouds that look like nuclear explosions in the distance or closer than the distance. I can duplicate the illusions of dark skies coming over the horizon and gas clouds moving toward the enemy.

"And that's what we have done. All of this has now been programmed by my team. The illusion is as believable as the view of Shenandoah Valley from this window. This window's view was done with the technology that existed in those years. These files are far superior." And he reached in his breast pocket of his suit and pulled out a small black plastic case.

"All of what I just described now exists on this external hard drive."

After a long quiet, Vice President Mapes asked, "Can you give us a demonstration here?"

"Yes, I can but I won't. President Jared told me last night that he didn't want to take a chance on a demonstration for him or anyone else because he isn't sure what the enemy knows about our capabilities or if they're able to delve into our system. There is no value to an extraneous preview. President Jared said that if he orders us to go ahead on this, sight unseen, it will either be effective or it will fail. If it is effective, it will speak for itself. If it fails, we will be no better off then before the order was given. Did I quote you right, Mister President?"

President Jared nodded. "You quoted me right on the nose, Mr. Stuart. Go on. Keep explaining."

"A friend of mine, Mort McClure, who is one of those who helped me on the political angle of all this, suggested to me that it's possible that in case of sudden attack on the United States, all contingency headquarters might be destroyed or beyond our ability to communicate depending on what the enemy would do. He was quite a prophet. Now I can't get hold of Mort. Maybe they killed him. He was an older guy who was once a low-level appointee with the Department of Defense back in the 1980s in the Reagan Administration and went on to travel the world throughout most of his adult life and knew people everywhere. Without telling him why—and he never asked—I told him I wanted a list of people he knew throughout the world who would have his absolute trust; who knew current technology and would keep up with it, and most of all, who would put liberty above all. He used eighteen months getting hold of individuals throughout various specified cities of the world and then compiled for me a list of their names and backgrounds and priority of trust, along with their computer codes. He gave me the list. I contacted the best of them as soon as we got wind that a crisis could be in store. I told them it was uncertain but to stand-by until they heard more from me, and to be in contact with chiefs of any of our armed forces in their local areas, if there were any. I don't want to give the impression that no one knows about all this, but no one knows about this in its entirety including its world-wide scope. I'm not even telling you all the cities involved. No reason to do that. Everything was on an absolute need-to-know basis but I have to admit, a lot of trust has gone into this."

Again he held up the small plastic case. "If these files are downloaded to those people throughout the world and if they can launch them correctly—I am certain they could cause panic of the enemy, and at a minimum the enemy can be disoriented and diverted, and if our own armed forces and allied armed forces still exist even in small numbers and then come into play, I believe and, more important, President Jared believes that some of the enemy revolutionary forces can be wiped out. It depends on our troop strength and our weaponry that might still exist and the ability of our armed forces and allied armed forces to take advantage of the moment. I repeat, that is—if some of our own armed forces and allied armed forces still exist. It's something we don't know. What we are doing is providing what President Jared calls the forward troops—the most massive and imaginary forward troops in history. Right behind them will be the real ones. The enemy does have to have someone to whom they can surrender.

"President Jared believes our armed forces *do* exist and are still fighting. If so, our underground knows how to contact them and *will* contact them as soon as they receive the files from me for them to download. Those chiefs of U.S. armed forces have already been contacted by our underground before the crisis began, on an 'only if it happens' basis. I re-contacted them just hours ago after meeting with President Jared—but still on a 'maybe' basis.

"Remember, these files don't have to be sent from here to any Contingency Headquarters or any Command Centers or anyone connected with any government. The people on the list are part of what we call our underground. We set up a private network. And it is operational. Of course, it goes up to and down from our satellites.

"Any time I'm directed to do it, I can send the computer files up to the satellites and then down to the names on the list, directing the underground members on the downloading instructions in line with their own topography, and also giving them instructions of how and when to launch them. They should all be launched by our underground simultaneously so the enemy has no time to investigate and notify others throughout the world of what's going on in their own locations. It all has to happen at once."

There was nothing but silence. No one felt worthy of touching what he said. And what he said was even more astonishing than the view that surrounded them for which he had been responsible.

President Jared interrupted the silence by saying, "If I did anything at all to help you, Wayne, it was to 'stand out of your light.' Wayne can have this thing sent off to the allied underground in thirty hours from my go-ahead. The only reason I didn't give him the order right away is that I wanted to wait until I read your advice in case any of it was better—and to give more opportunity for President Wadsworth or anyone in the constitutional line of succession to make it known they are alive and able to make decisions as president. None of your advice was better, and President Wadsworth still hasn't presented himself nor did anyone in the constitutional line of succession."

Secretary Brendon asked, "Wayne, doesn't there have to be white screens set up at all these locales?"

"No. You're thinking of projection. These are digital images that are not projected. If you want to think of it this way—the program offers a black screen, not a white one—it blocks out the real image that's ahead of the viewer. What is really in front of them becomes blotted out; a shield that produces a transition to a new sky, a new foreground, thousands of separate pictures from which the people we send the download can choose. I will instruct them on what I think is best for their circumstance but it will be up to them. They will have a lot of choice of topography, armies, explosions, everything and practically anything they want to be viewed. That's just a quick way to think of what this is. It is called augmented reality. I call my version a digital mask."

Secretary Anderson turned to President Jared. "What's this got to do with missile defense?"

Wayne Stuart took the initiative to answer for the President. "What I just said has nothing to do with missile defense. President Jared was just trying to explain what gave him the satellite idea to—"

"Don't bother explaining it, Mr. Stuart. Forget it, Anderson. Now, let me ask all of you: give me your vote. You don't have to understand it. You have to believe in it. It's what Mr. Stuart said. It's a digital mask. Do I give Mr. Stuart the order to go ahead? Remember, a 'yes' vote means in thirty hours he sends the programs out to the underground. Let's go around the room, one by one."

"Absolutely."

"I should say, sir."

"Do it!"

"I'm on. Do it."

"Positive."

"I'm for it, Mister President."

"Of course."

"Yoh!"

"As you said, sir, there is no down-side to going ahead."

Eli Jared nodded. "Did I say that? Yes, I guess I did." And he looked at Wayne Stuart. "Then I'll give you your order. Go ahead, Wayne. And we thank you for six years of very dedicated work. And let's hope it pays off in victory."

"Thank you, Mister President."

"One other thing, Wayne. I vote for accusing you of insubordination. You didn't tell the Congress, you didn't tell the State Department, you didn't tell anyone in a D.C. bureaucracy and, in fact, you lied to government officials about what projects on which you were spending taxpayer's money. So you stand accused of obstruction of justice, contempt of the congress, and perjury. And you even confessed to those crimes—in front of all these witnesses in this room. However, out of the kindness of my heart I am now also exercising my ability as Acting President to give you a full presidential pardon. Now, Mr. Stuart, since you're a free man again—go ahead and win the war."

Wayne Stuart was smiling. "Yes, sir."

"Gentlemen, not one word about this to anyone. This is strictly on a need-to-know basis. No one other than those in ExCom 2 of which Wayne Stuart is now a member, should be told one hint of this. None of us know what the revolutionaries will do in the next thirty hours. Understood?"

There was a unanimous "yes" and "understood."

"And so ahead of us is a countdown for some thirty hours requiring our patience while Wayne does his magic. To borrow a timekeeping phrase from our missile and space exploration terminology it is now—" and he looked at his watch and clicked a button by its bezel—"T Minus 30 Hours."

"No, Mister President," Wayne Stuart interjected quickly. "T-Time should be the time of launch. In thirty hours I should be able to send the programs out. Then the underground needs to have eight days before they *launch* the programs. That's important because there's too much for them to do and too much can go wrong. The time of launch has to be coordinated so that, as I said, every launch is simultaneous with the others. They need eight days. I have already given them the warning to standby, but no more than that because I needed your go-ahead. When I send the programs they need the eight days I told them they would get."

"So we're talking about another eight days after your thirty hours before these things are launched?"

"Yes, sir."

"God, that's a lot."

"Yes, sir."

"Quicker!"

"That will be difficult, sir."

"Everything is difficult, Wayne. Everything. It has to be quicker. Every second that passes, people are being killed. Maybe every second thousands of people are being killed. More people are being tortured. We know that. Every second. Wayne, you have given this six years. Now every second means human misery."

"Yes, sir."

"What can you do to make it quicker?"

"I can't give them less time after receiving the programs."

"How about six days rather than eight?"

"It's taking a chance. That's quite a reduction of time for them."

"Let's take the chance. Now, what can you do to reduce *your* time before sending it off?"

"If they have to cut their time, I can cut mine. I'll cut three hours from my thirty hours. Twenty-seven hours for me. I put in some safety for myself. I'll cut three hours from my time."

"Six."

"Cut my time by six hours?"

"Six. That will give you an even twenty-four. Can you do it, Wayne?"

"So that's twenty-four hours from now until the time of no return. Once the programs are sent out, that's it."

"That's right."

"Six days after that until launch."

"That's right."

"We'll do it, sir."

"You're not going to get much sleep, are you?"

"I planned on not sleeping for a long time. Now I can go to sleep a little earlier. I'm expecting some troubles after they receive them:

some complaints from one of the underground who won't be able to download it. Or for one reason or another won't be able to launch it at the right time. Things like that can happen."

Eli Jared nodded. "So what's the new schedule? Repeat it, Wayne, so I get it straight."

"I'll send off the programs in twenty-four hours. They'll launch them six days from then. So it's a total of 171 hours. No, no. That's not right. I was originally going to have thirty hours and they were going to have eight days so that was a total of—"

Vice President Mapes said, "Wait, Wayne, wait. You just made a simple mathematical mistake. You said thirty hours at first when you should have ended up figuring twenty-four. So you said—"

Eli Jared said, "Alright. Alright. I don't care what anyone said at first. So what is it?"

Wayne said, "In twenty-four hours from now I'll send it off. In six days from that time will be T-Time all over the world. So that's whatever six times twenty-four is plus another twenty-four. Right?"

Vice President Mapes nodded. "That makes 168 hours total. Or, as you say, T-Time will be 168 hours from now."

"Actually, it's more accurate to start the clock when I get out of this Solarium and into my office." He looked at his watch. "Let me start the countdown clock at 8:30 a.m."

Eli Jared looked confused. "Look, do me a favor, Wayne. I'm an old man. I can't count all these hours and things. Make your T-Time when you launch the programs to all the world-wide posts, so I can figure this thing out. Then when that's done start a new launch cycle for the six days. So when you start your count, just call it T minus twenty-four hours. Can you do that for an old man?"

Wayne Stuart nodded with his frequent smile. "I can do that for a man of any age, Mister President."

Secretary of the Interior Houghton said, "Mister President?"

"Yes, Houghton?"

Secretary Houghton was probably the most knowledgeable expert on the natural resources of the United States, and for that reason he was selected by Eli Jared to be on ExCom 2. He didn't seem to know much about anything other than natural resources and he seemed to be drifting at this meeting. He was a man with eternally sleepy eyes with lips extending downwards at both tips as if to say, 'Oh, I don't know. What's the use? Who cares?' This time he said, "This is a good step, Mister President." Then his lips went back to their usual disinterested downward position.

Eli Jared looked confused and said, "Profound! Profound!" Then he looked at back at Wayne Stuart. "Wayne, whenever you want you can be excused. Thank you. I mean that more than I can adequately express. Thank you, Wayne. And when you get to your office we will have twenty-four hours until—for all intents and purposes it is—whatever you said—passing the line of no return. Right?"

"That's right, Mister President."

"Then once we pass that mark we wait for six days from then—that will be a new T-Time. Right?"

"Yes, that's correct."

"That's right. Now," and he looked around the room. "Mapes?"

"Yes, sir," Vice President Mapes responded.

"You seem to be good at mathematics, Mapes. This is simple stuff—this isn't Einstein, so I want you to figure it all out for me so I can follow it on my watch. I need times. Exact times. Our time here in Virginia. I'll know what time it is here when Waync is going to press the button, but I want to know what time it will be for the next launch when the buttons are pressed around the world—our time on regular human watches."

"Yes, sir."

"That will be good." And he scanned the room. "We now have a long period to hope and pray that nothing catastrophic happens. Any other ideas that we can enact, I want to hear them. I still want to hear them. One idea doesn't preclude others. As I told you before, I don't want ideas on how we can die; I can think of a million of those. I want ideas on how the United States and the rest of civilized societies can *live.* No matter that we have this magnificent, innovative and creative idea or if we have a number of ideas, let's always search for more. And through all of this, we hope—we pray—that President Wadsworth is alive and well and is giving directives that win the war, making our efforts expendable and unnecessary."

CHAPTER

9

Countdown

T Minus 22 Hours 03 Minutes and Counting: (10:27 a.m. EDT)

The quarters of Secretary Desmond were outrageously unkempt, but he didn't notice. There were piles of new cellophane-enclosed shirts, underwear, and socks on the floor. There were scattered papers lying near them, and there were cardboard boxes on chairs, some of them sealed and some of them tipped and open with nothing in them. On the coffee table were three slices of pizza that looked like they were there for an extended period of time. Secretary Desmond was sitting on the edge of his unmade bed in pajamas and a bathrobe. A visitor was sitting on one of his rocking chairs. The rocking chairs had been sent to him by Dr. Rubins at the Sebotus Hospital. "Don't you think I should be going to a cabinet meeting? Why doesn't Jared call a cabinet meeting?"

Secretary Desmond's visitor was Angus Glass who seemed to be the only one who cared about such questions of Secretary Desmond. "Yes, I do think the cabinet should be involved in everything that's going on, Mister President. But there's been no cabinet meeting because I don't think anything is going on. Jared isn't doing anything. Like you, I'm on the cabinet, and no one knows what's going on. There is no leadership. That's what's going on."

"Don't call me Mister President, my friend. I'm not president."

"I wouldn't be so sure, Mister President."

"I am not president because I was born in Bermuda of all places." Secretary Desmond, at least for this moment, was softer and more measured than he was when he entered Sebotus Headquarters three nights ago.

"How do you know?"

"How do I know what?"

"How do you know you were born in Bermuda?"

"I was there."

"You mean you remember your birth?"

"Of course not. No one remembers their birth. Where were *you* born? What's your name?"

"I was born in Petaluma, California, Mister President, and I am Acting Secretary of Housing and Urban Development, Angus Glass."

"So you're Angus Glass then. You don't remember being born in wherever you said you were born, do you?"

"Petaluma. No, I don't. But I know I was. I remember being brought up there. Mister President, you told me you don't know one thing about Bermuda."

"Why do you keep calling me Mister President? Whether I remember Bermuda or not, I was born there. Hamilton. Hamilton, Bermuda. That's what my birth certificate says. That's on my passport. That's on everything. My parents and I came to the States when I was an infant."

"Who told you that? Eli Jared?"

"Admiral Kaylin."

"Where's your birth certificate? Where's your passport?"

"I don't know where my birth certificate is."

"And your passport?"

"I don't know."

"Mister President, you don't know where anything is. You have amnesia. I think they induced your amnesia. I think they doped you up and you're still doped up."

"I remember a lot of things."

"I think they doped you up to have selective amnesia. Is that what it's called? I don't understand such things. I don't take any medication. But I know that you, Mister President, can remember some things, but you don't seem to remember things that have real relevance to you. Who's your wife?"

He was stumped.

"Who's your wife, Mister President?"

Secretary Desmond stared at Angus Glass.

"What's your address—your home address?"

He shook his head. "I don't remember the number, but it's in Gettysburg."

"In Gettysburg!?"

"Yes."

"The Gettysburg Address?"

"No, no, no. I don't live there now. I was born in Gettysburg. Gettysburg, Pennsylvania."

It was Angus Glass's turn to stare. "I see."

"I remember playing—we used to play in the battlefield. My friends were Tommy Luft and Roger—Roger Cassidy. See how I remember?"

"Mister President, were you born in Gettysburg before or after you were born in Bermuda?"

"After. After. I grew up in Gettysburg but I was born in Hamilton, Bermuda."

"What hospital?"

"I don't know. Admiral Kaylin didn't tell me."

"I see. Admiral Kaylin didn't tell you?"

"That's right."

"Has he become your biographer and your doctor?"

"No. Not at all."

"Mister President, let me tell you something. As you might know, the Internet is inoperative—stopped by the revolutionary government. No search engines or anything except what some Imam is saying. Revolutionary material. But in our library here—which doesn't have much—just a few books—there is a World Almanac. It's an old one. I found a very short biography of you when you were CEO of Madison Mutual."

"I was?"

"Yes. You were—just before you were appointed as Secretary of Commerce by President Wadsworth. You know what it says?"

"What?"

"What if I were to tell you that it says you were born in Milwaukee, Wisconsin?"

"Is that what it says?"

"No. Not exactly. It says that your first job was when you were 12 years old at WISN Radio station in Milwaukee hosting a show called 'Just Kids.'"

"Huh! I think I remember that!"

"Mister President, you were not born in Bermuda. At that meeting in the Lucite Room you said you were born in Bermuda—and that your parents were British. You said that because I'm sure that's what you were told—and then you added that you were brought up in Milwaukee, Pennsylvania. I think you meant Milwaukee, Wisconsin and Wisconsin is a state of the United States."

"That's right."

"And then maybe you moved to Gettysburg, Pennsylvania. I don't think you get it, sir. You are the President of the United States, sir. And you were stripped of your presidency by Kaylin who I am sure was part of a conspiracy. And I'll bet it was all to get Eli Jared into that office so he could be President, or appear to be. But you are the President."

"Huh!"

"And you should claim your office."

"Good gracious!"

"Jared is not in the constitutional line for the presidency."

"Good gracious alive!"

"And I think you ought to make it known that you know. I can't tell them I know because if I tell them, they'll kill me."

"Good gracious alive. What's your name again?"

"Acting Secretary of Housing and Urban Development Angus Glass."

"That's right."

"I think you should tell them you know."

"But then—won't they kill *me*? If they'd kill *you*, won't they kill *me*?"

Angus Glass hesitated. Then he gave a slow nod. "Yeah. I think so. That's a valid point."

"Then what do we do?"

"I don't know who's in on it. I don't know who to trust and who not to trust."

"What do we do?"

"I'll think of something, sir. That's my job. I'm going to give you back your constitutional role. That's what my job is. I can feel it."

"You think you can do that while saving my life at the same time? I would like my life to be saved."

"I'll do that."

"If you do that, you can be my Vice President—can't you?"

There was a look of amazement on Angus Glass's face. "Well, yes. Of course it is totally up to you, Mister President. I'm sure I can handle that for you, sir. I would serve at the pleasure of the president."

It seemed to Angus Glass that fate was playing a large hand in his future career. There was, of course, some difficulty in his analysis of the birthplace of Secretary Desmond, as well as the authority of Secretary Desmond to appoint a Vice President.

T Minus 19 Hours 17 Minutes and Counting: (1:13 p.m. EDT)

The Recreation Room had dozens of misplaced chairs and a television set that was turned on but showed nothing more than a backlit gray screen. There were magazine racks filled with old magazines printed before the success of the revolutionaries, and there were seven women sitting in a circle. People who work in places of hundreds or thousands always find a way to form smaller groups, and times of tension call for them to be formed quickly. These women had formed their smaller group shortly after the crisis began and they had all been selected from the staff to be the "utility players" of Sebotus members. Their rank as staff members had suddenly elevated them into an exclusive circle of camaraderie.

Traci Howe was there and so was Helen Peterson, and there was Anna, Susan, Jennifer, Elsie, and Kate.

Susan, the Assistant to Acting Attorney General Jonathan Hynd asked, "Is there something going on that we don't know?"

As if there wasn't enough to worry about, this question struck Traci hard. Was it known what she did last night? How could anyone have found out that she had been in the Solarium with Admiral Kaylin?

She almost said, "I just brought him some dinner" when she caught herself after she heard the first two words come out of her mouth. "I just—don't know. What do you just mean?" Too many "justs" but it was better than what she was going to say.

The strangeness of her response wasn't noticed or, at least, it didn't bother Susan. "I think something is going on that we're not being told. I think there's some move that's going to be made and I don't know what it is."

"Really?" Traci asked with pretended interest and unattempted relief. Traci controlled her innate instinct to tell them all about her new relationship with Admiral Kaylin since, as a woman talking to other women, she was tempted to reveal a personal problem to selected others, not seeking a solution but wanting to make her dilemma the center of their discussion. In this case, however, her strength and good sense overrode that distinctive feminine characteristic.

Helen shook her head. "We're not being paid to know anything. What makes you think some big move is going to be made, honey?"

"It's just a feeling," Susan answered as best she could. "Attorney General Hynd came back from a meeting this morning like he was in a trance. It was different. Margot's voice came over the speaker earlier this morning and announced there would be a meeting of something I never heard of before. So I didn't pay any attention to it. The speaker announcements play in his office so if he had any interest he would tell me. *Normally* he would tell me, anyway. He left the office and didn't tell me why or where he was going, and when he came back he was in a trance. Now, I'm exaggerating. It wasn't a real trance but he was different. I think he looked excited—he looked excited; even happy. I haven't seen him look excited or happy since he came here. Something is going on. I just feel it. Do you know what I mean?"

"Yes," Anna said. "I know what you mean. Where's the Solarium?"

Traci gave a slight jolt in her chair. When she realized her body had made a motion she asked, "The Solarium? What's that?"

Anna nodded, "I heard Margot on the speaker this morning too, and she told some group to meet at the Solarium at eight o'clock. I never heard of it before. That's probably what you heard, Susan."

Susan asked, "Did Secretary Bayler leave for the meeting?"

"He did leave, yes. I don't know if he went to that meeting."

Anna wouldn't leave it alone. "Didn't he tell you anything?"

"No. He didn't say a word before he left or after he came back. But that's not unusual for him. He doesn't talk much."

"Maybe that's enough," Kate said. "We shouldn't be asking questions. That's not our business. Whatever it is—we'll find out."

"Did Secretary Wilson go to that meeting? Did he leave the office at eight o'clock?" Anna asked.

Kate pursed her lips and answered, "I don't know. I wasn't even in the office at that time. I went to the cafeteria. I wanted some breakfast, so I don't know." And then as if to prove she wasn't lying she added, "Corn flakes." No one had asked her for evidence.

Anna went back to the subject she had addressed with persistence. "So what's the Solarium?"

"A meeting room, I guess," Susan answered. "I don't think it's a hot tub!"

There was some giggling and a curious look by Traci who then started laughing to join the crowd.

T Minus 16 Hours 40 Minutes and Counting: (3:50 p.m. EDT)

It was not the same in Admiral Kaylin's office nor could it be since the event of the night before in the Solarium. Traci sat in her outer office intoxicated with passion, excitement, sickness, and conscience all in one unexpected package. Now when her intercom buzzed from his contact, she hesitated before answering him, her mind racing, and then saying what she had to say, "Yes, Admiral?" Those two words that had nothing but a robotic meaning a day ago now created a giant wave in her stomach.

There was an equal mix of feelings on the other end although Admiral Kaylin hid it with faked composure almost as well as she did. They were two bad actors who could have fooled no one but each other. 'Is she sorry?' he thought.

'Was it nothing more than a one-night stand for him?' she thought. 'The circumstances made me look prettier to him last night than I am to him now, and now he wants it stopped.'

"Traci, could I see you for a moment?"

Now her stomach took a dip below all laws of anatomical possibility. "You want me to come in, Admiral?"

"Yes. Please."

She made a quick decision not to even look in a mirror. After all, she had never done that before when called into her boss's office. But she did it, anyway. Decisions quickly made were inconsequential.

She went into his adjoining office and she was even conscious of her walk. So was he. And then he pretended to take a quick scan of some paper on his desk. He looked up from it and said in his most formal voice, "Sit down, Traci."

She sat on the chair across from his desk. That's when he noticed she had taken a notebook and pen with her and she put the notebook on her crossed legs as though she was ready to write down whatever he was going to say.

"No dictation; no notes, Traci."

She looked piercingly at him.

"Traci—" and he couldn't think of what to say even though he had decided what to say.

"You want to say you're sorry for last night? Go ahead. I understand. I'm sorry, too. Just forget it, Admiral. I can."

Admiral Kaylin shook his head. "No, you can't and neither can I. That isn't what I was going to say. Traci, I am—I am so taken with you that I can't think straight."

It was as though the giant wave that she thought was going to drown her had suddenly gone out to sea, leaving her unhurt. "You are?"

He nodded. "I am. Traci, I—" Any plan of being articulate was as gone as Traci's wave.

She got up from her chair and walked to his side of the desk. It was brave, but she had always been brave. "Admiral Kaylin, in the midst of this world nightmare, it was the most wonderful evening of my life."

He nodded. "I feel that way, Traci. And since then it gives me another reason to hope that we all live."

That statement made her fight back tears. "I've never been so frightened, I've never been so happy, I've never felt so terrible, I've never felt so guilty, and I've never felt so right. Do you know what I mean? Do you—Admiral?"

"Traci, do you think you could call me Keith? Calling me Admiral is much too formal now," and he smiled.

She shook her head. "I must call you Admiral. Otherwise I'll make a slip and say your first name and then everyone will know."

"Why should we care?"

"Because we *should* care. I work for you."

"Why, Traci? What difference will it make to anyone?"

"You're my boss. I think it will make a difference."

"To who?"

"To the President." And she quickly felt she made a mistake in saying that.

"Jared? Why would he care?"

She shook her head. "I'm just thinking of what he has on his mind every moment with his responsibility, and I think this would bother him—and that's not good. His mind has to be free."

Admiral Kaylin put a hand to his forehead and started rubbing it casually. "I still don't get it, Traci. Does he have—affection for you? Is that what you mean?"

"No, I don't mean that! He's an old man—Admiral. And he's such a wonderful old man. Even if he felt a touch of what you said—affection—he would never let me know."

He stared at her a while without saying a word. Then he asked, "Then how would you know if he did?"

"Because a woman always knows. A woman knows even if it comes from a boy that's too young or a man that's too old. A woman always knows. But he isn't thinking that way. But I think it could hurt him to think there was anything between you and me, that's all. So that's all. He has enough on his mind."

Admiral Kaylin nodded. "I wouldn't want to hurt him any more than you would. I wouldn't take the chance."

"Then I'll continue to call you Admiral. Besides, I like saying Admiral. Don't you like it?"

He nodded. "Somehow, I think I do. I think it's the way you say it."

"You think?"

T Minus 12 Hours 02 Minutes and Counting: (8:28 p.m. EDT)

Wayne Stuart sat on the other side of the coffee table from Eli Jared in Eli Jared's apartment. The table was filled with papers, pads, coffee cups and there was a small clock. "This is important, Wayne. This is terribly important. How much can you trust all these contacts of yours throughout the world?"

"I don't know them. I don't know any of them. Mort McClure, who I suspect is dead, is the one who lined them up. It took him a year and a half to line up these people. As for Mr. McClure—he was as trustworthy as any a man I ever knew. And politically—he would have given his life in a moment for this country. That's why I think he's dead. He was threatened by Islamist revolutionaries back in the 1980s. They had a price on his head then."

"Well then, this will be a tribute to Mort. But what I'm going to ask has a great deal of risk to it. You told me that those people—your underground—were told by you to contact our chiefs of U.S. military in their local area about the plan when you gave them the stand-by, right?"

"I did."

"And if there were no U.S. armed forces in their area?"

"Then they couldn't tell anyone."

"How many of them have U.S. forces in the area?"

"Out of the eighty contacts, forty-two of them are right here in the United States. Out of the other thirty-eight, I would say somewhere between twenty and twenty-five *should* have U.S. forces there. I'm not certain of the exact number."

"I want you to do this: Take notes on this, Wayne. Here —" and he slid a yellow legal pad across the table to Wayne Stuart. "You have a pencil?"

Wayne Stuart reached for the pad and took a ball-point pen from his shirt pocket. "Yes, sir. A pen."

"Take notes, Wayne. I'll talk slow. I want you to do this: tell only those underground contacts who have U.S. armed forces in their areas to notify the Chief of our armed forces—the U.S. forces in their area—to plan as massive an offensive as they can put together for the precise moment after the digital mask, as you call it, is launched by the underground. And when I say a massive offense,

I mean massive. For overseas sites, our armed forces can and should use *every* means available to them to make the offensive successful. I don't care what kind of weaponry they use. I don't care how few armed forces are still there; your program will make them seem endless—we hope. In the other countries that don't have U.S. forces, don't tell them a thing about this unless Vice President Mapes tells you he knows for sure that the particular country's military and Chief of State are totally with us. No moderates; no maybes. I'll tell Mapes to visit with you. But if he says to do it, then do it, even though their foreigners. Mapes is a knowledgeable fellow; used to be with the National Security Council. He's so knowledgeable on foreign policy that Wadsworth made him both Acting National Security Advisor and Acting Vice President. Got that so far, Wayne?"

Wayne Stuart finished writing a sentence and then looked up from his pad. "Yes, sir."

"Good. Can I go on?"

"Yes, sir. Please."

"Now then, in the cases where your underground contact is dealing with our own armed forces either here or overseas, tell your contact to tell our Chief of the armed forces in the local area that the offensive is an *order* from the Commander in Chief—from the Acting President of the United States. If it's an allied force approved by Mapes, tell whoever it is that it's a *request* from the Acting President of the United States. Got it? And I want your underground to tell the U.S. or allied armed forces about this *personally*. No emails, no telephones, no electronics. As for the other countries with neither U.S. nor friendly forces, don't tell your contact anything beyond what he has to know about the digital mask. There is risk. Some may not believe my authority. Some may not believe yours. I don't know who they can contact to verify anything at this point. All of this is going to rely on those who have the weaponry and troops and understand the peril of our times—and have the guts to do what must be done. And they'll know it if they use their heads—and if they use their hearts. It will be a gamble for them. It's a gamble for all of us. We're all working in the blind.

"Admiral Kaylin knows about all this and that's important to let our forces know about his involvement as Acting Chairman of the Joint Chiefs of Staff, if they know who that is. That's it: there's you, Mapes, Kaylin, and me. Everything understood, Wayne?"

Wayne Stuart finished writing the item about Mapes, and stopped writing to look squarely at Eli Jared. "Mister President, when you say those overseas should use any weaponry to make their offensive successful, are you including or excluding nuclear weapons?"

"Everything is included. It depends on what's necessary. As you know, your digital mask serves as the forward troops—even the forward earth. The live who coordinate with your digital mask have to be willing to use everything they have to bring white flags waving from poles held by the enemy. To bring this about, nuclear weapons are included. The only exclusion is defeat."

T Minus 10 Hours and Counting:
(10:30 p.m. EDT)

With the volume turned low, the television monitor in Eli Jared's apartment was on and Eli Jared faced it as he sat on his bed.

"Allahu Akhbar! God is Great! This is IFRA's Nightly News of the Islamic Fundamentalist Republic of America. God, hasten the arrival of Imam al-Mahdi and grant him good health and victory, and make us his followers who attest to his rightfulness." Young and pretty starlets were shown, each with lips purple-red from dried blood after razorblades were used to remove their lipstick by the authorities. In a videotape from earlier in the evening, Hollywood Boulevard was closed to traffic between Orange and Highland for what was described as a celebration for the motion picture industry at the Kodak Theater. Only men from the industry were invited to the black-tie event with none expecting the speech that was given by an Imam who chastised them for their on-screen and off-screen depravity. He went on to inform them that all screenplays must be submitted to the Revolutionary Law and Order Council for approval before production of any future film could begin. As the guests from the motion picture industry were dismissed from the theater, the most well known of them were herded to a separate room off the lobby area. Their limousine drivers who had parked their vehicles on Yucca Street were waiting for the cue to pick up their passengers but instead were instructed by the authorities to leave without them. The former celebrities were herded together and led somewhere else by truck while a loudspeaker told them "Allahu Akhbar! God is Great!"

The telecast did not end but went to New Delhi, India. The screen showed the huge circular shopping center of Connaught Circus while the Imam narrator spoke about justice being done to Hindus and also to Moslems who rejected and had fought against the revolution. One after another, men in their ethnic attire of dhotis and kurtas with their hands tied behind their backs and blindfolds over their eyes, were thrown from the precipice of the Odeon Theater onto the inner circle street, and from the precipice of the Kashmir Government Art Emporium. Then the scene changed to the National Stadium where young women were brought into the stadium by the truckload. Each woman was separately buried up to her neck and stoned to death as the narrator spoke about the crime of adultery.

"Allahu Akhbar!" The off-screen narrator said.

CHAPTER

10

Traci's Prayer

T Minus 9 Hours 19 Minutes and Counting: (11:11 p.m. EDT)

Ever since the crisis began, the Chapel was a place of unscheduled entrances and exits and entrances again of human traffic. It was a chapel unlike any other place of worship. Behind the altar was a row of painted sculptures: Moses holding the Ten Commandments; Jesus on the crucifix; a crowned Mohammed on his prayer rug; a sitting golden Buddha; a first incarnation of the Hindu God, Vishnu; and a standing Confucius, his hands clasped below his chest. On the walls were two huge murals of religious figures of Taoism, Zoroastrianism, and Bahai faiths, and depictions of religions most Americans didn't recognize. Only atheists would not be comfortable in this place of worship but they wouldn't be in the Chapel anyway.

There was a Chaplain who had a slight Irish brogue and that in itself was a comfort to some of those who would talk to him.

Beyond standing at the altar he would often walk among the seated and ever-changing congregation and he would sit with one and then another and then another. He talked with some, held hands with some, and prayed with those who wanted his voice or just his silent presence beside them.

At this time of night Chaplain Ryan wasn't there because if he was he would almost be by himself in the Chapel. But Traci was there, sitting in the second row of pews surrounded by no one. Maybe it was the best time for her to come to the Chapel because the loneliness of its interior at this hour made her feel closer to the Recipient of her prayer.

"God, please make our people safe. Please. Please make us win this war. And God, I know you have a lot to do right now, and a lot of prayers to listen to, and I don't want to bother you, so just one quick question that's personal if you have time. If you don't, then don't listen to the rest of this. As I'm sure you know, Eli Jared is Acting President of the United States—our country. I don't want to give him any difficulty. But I'm very fond—I mean *very* fond—I *love* Admiral Kaylin who is so important to President Jared. You probably know that Admiral Kaylin and I have been together and that life may be going away from both of us. I'm not so sure President Jared would like us seeing each other. So my question to you is this: Do you want me to stop seeing Admiral Kaylin? I mean I *work* for him so I can't actually stop *seeing* him, but should I stop seeing him in *that* way? Or, God, should I stay with him no matter what? If the world should end, I want to die with him. What do you think? I don't want to add to President Jared's problems. He is now the most important man in the whole world. And more important than anything I'm saying, is to please help him and make sure our nation survives and our people are made safe and happy again. And that we win. And that all the *good* people in the world are out of danger, please. I know that's what you're trying to do. But if you have time, going back to what I was saying originally about things here with Admiral Kaylin and what I should do—these may be our last days of life here on Earth, God. Can you please tell me what to do, if you have the time? Don't go through any trouble. I mean it. Can you tell me? Do you think you can tell me by giving me a sign? Wait. Wait, please. There's something else you should know. President Jared is such a great man, and as you know, he's old. And he teases me, just in fun about me being pretty. It's all just teasing and fun—but I think he might feel something for me. You know you made me in a way that I can tell those things. Maybe he doesn't; maybe he's just flattering me; he's a big flatterer of people at times, but if he does feel something for me, then it increases my—my dilemma. And maybe your dilemma, too. Now, if you can, can you please give me a sign so I know what to do? Any sign will do." Then she added, "and would be appreciated."

If God was a man He would probably have fallen in love with her, Himself. And He was even older than Eli Jared.

Traci sat there for a while, hoping to get a sign while she was still there. 'No matter,' she thought. 'I have to give God time.' She got up slowly and walked to the end of the line of empty pews in which she had sat and then she walked up the aisle to the exit. As she got to the door she saw she was not alone in the Chapel. There was a man in the last row of pews. His head was bent. He was in prayer. He was an old man. He did not look up, but even though it was dark and his head was bent down quite far, she recognized him easily as he was the most important man in the world.

"What does that sign mean, God?" she asked as she left the Chapel. "Could you please give me another one?"

CHAPTER

11

In the Countdown Room

T Minus 0 Hours 12 minutes and Counting: (8:18 a.m. EDT)

"Wayne Stuart is on the line, Mister President."

It was a sentence that Eli Jared both hoped and feared Helen Peterson would announce. It was 8:18 in the morning and the schedule called for Wayne Stuart to send off the programs in twelve minutes. Eli Jared gave a short clasp of his hands and then released his hands to pick up the phone. "Wayne?"

"Yes, sir, Mister President."

"Are we A-OK?"

"We're okay, sir."

"Wonderful! Wonderful! Thank you, Wayne. Thank you."

"I thought you might like to be here, sir, when I push the send-switch."

"Oh, you bet! But I hope I won't be standing in your light."

"No, sir. I want you here. You have every right to be here."

"I'll be there in a minute—as fast as the elevator can take me."

Wayne's office looked like the control room of the most modern and well-equipped television network news facility combined with NASA's Central Control. There were eighty monitors on the wall forming a huge rectangle of eight rows down by ten across, all monitors having a separate digital clock beneath them. Above the monitors was a map of the world with a white LED light at each of the designated sites. In front of that wall was a massive black console with dozens of rheostat controls running vertically and hundreds of different colored keyboard buttons. Sitting at the console, like a master conductor of an orchestra with instruments totally dependent on his touch that could send them into glory or oblivion, was Wayne Stuart.

He turned around in his chair when the door opened by Eli Jared's unrestricted pass. Wayne Stuart stood up.

"Sit down. Sit down, boy," Eli Jared said breathlessly.

"That's okay. Sit down here, sir. I put a chair next to mine and you can not only watch the moment, but you can push the send-switch when I give you the signal."

"No, no, no. I'd botch it all up. You do it. But I would like to sit next to you and just watch what you do. You don't need to explain anything." Eli Jared walked to Wayne Stuart and both of them sat down facing the huge console.

"Let me just explain what's going on here, sir. These monitors that are black right now—no image—are the eighty locations around the world. Forty-two of them are major cities in the United States and, as you know, the other thirty-eight are major cities of friendly nations around the world. I know you like to think in our time—in Eastern Daylight Time, but the clocks are all set to each city's local time and when the send-switch is pressed all clocks revert to Greenwich time in those cities. We have to be on a single time all over the world once it gets to the underground. That first monitor on the top left is London and, of course, London is already on Greenwich time. Right now our time here at Sebotus is 8:22 Eastern Daylight Time. That clock on the north wall is a countdown clock showing hours, minutes and seconds counting down to T-Time. In other words, see those ticking seconds?"

"Yes, yes."

"It says 0 hours, 8 minutes and 43 seconds. Now 42. Now 41. Now 40. Then, in—39 seconds now it will turn to 0 hours, 7 minutes, and 59 seconds. When it reads zero hours, zero minutes, zero seconds, I push the send-switch."

"Got it. What do we see when you do that?"

"All the monitors will turn on. Don't expect to see Big Ben, Times Square, and the Taj Mahal. You'll see unimposing shots of small rooms, usually in houses, and people you've never seen before fiddling with computer-keys, buttons, switches, and controls."

T Minus 0 Hours 0 minutes 16 Seconds and Counting: (8:29 a.m. EDT)

Wayne Stuart took a deep breath. "15 seconds. 14. 13. 12. 11. 10. 9. 8. 7. 6. 5. 4. 3. 2. 1. *Zee*-ro," and Wayne pressed the send-switch.

And nothing happened.

Wayne Stuart motioned his head to view every rheostat on his console, every computer control, every button, knob, switch, and back and forth at the totally dark monitors and the north-wall countdown clock that was stuck at T Minus 0 Hours 0 Minutes 0 Seconds.

Eli Jared's head was moving to follow every motion of Wayne Stuart's head and eyes. It was as though they were connected with Eli Jared on a short delay. "What's up? What's up? What's going on?"

Wayne Stuart's head and eyes did not stop their motions. "I don't know."

Eli Jared stopped his copying of Wayne Stuart's motions. "What's up, Stuart?"

This time Wayne Stuart didn't even answer him.

"I said, what's up, Stuart?"

"Can't talk, Mister President. Can't talk. We're on a hold. It's a hold. We're holding."

"Is it a built-in hold?"

"No. I don't have any built-in holds."

"Can you fix it?"

"Not if we keep talking."

Eli Jared stood up and started pacing the room. "This is horseradish! This is God awful! This is the fate of our country! This is the future of the world! This is the most important action of world history for God's sake."

Wayne Stuart paid no attention, or tried to pay no attention to anything Eli Jared was saying. His concentration was on switches and dials and monitors and clocks.

"Stuart! For God's sake, we put the lives of millions in your hands. I had faith. I had faith, boy. I don't know what the blue-blazes I was thinking. This is a tragedy! This can't even compete with other tragedies! Was I crazy? I put everything in your hands!"

"Sit down, Mister President, and be quiet."

He sat down. And he was quiet.

T Minus 0 Hours 0 minutes 0 Seconds and Holding: (8:30 a.m. EDT to 9:02 a.m. EDT)

A little more than a half-hour had passed spent in absolute silence except for an occasional click of a button. Neither Eli Jared nor Wayne Stuart said a word. Then, at 9:02 a.m. EDT Wayne Stuart made a sweep of his hand as he yelled "T-Time!" and pressed the send-switch again. And the room was bathed in light and color and moving images on monitors and animated digits of the countdown clock as well as increasing numbers escalating on all the clocks below the monitors. The room was a sudden host to a brilliant spectacle.

Wayne Stuart leaned back in his chair as he placed both hands behind his head. "T Plus 5 Seconds *and* Counting!" (9:02 a.m. EDT) "Now it's in *their* hands. Six days to go for them and now *they're* counting! It's 5:02 p.m. in London! Or 17:02!"

Eli Jared stood up. "Take it away, Rosedale, and buck up a buckaroo! Oh, my God, you did it, Wayne! You did it, you did it! How did you do it, boy?"

"I did what I should have done a half hour ago. I just re-booted the whole system. I turned it off and turned it on."

"That's all?"

"That's all."

"But how did that computer lock-up, or whatever it was, happen in the first place?"

Wayne Stuart shrugged. "Bill Gates. I guess he's entitled to make one mistake."

"A genius. A genius. I knew you were a genius. I always said you were a genius."

Wayne Stuart turned to him in his chair with a big closed-mouth smile on his face, his head still relaxed in his hands that formed a pillow for him. "Mister President, just minutes ago, I thought you were going to have my head! And I apologize for being rude to you, sir."

"I deserved it. You said what you had to say, son. I committed the sin of which I never wanted to be guilty. I stood in your light."

"No you didn't, sir. There is no way you could do that. You *are* my light."

CHAPTER

12

Tchavadar Dey

IT WAS CONSISTENTLY more active than the Chapel and the library and the recreation room and sometimes even more active than the cafeteria. The room had ten stationary bicycles, two treadmills, a fair number of small duo-handled devices and weights to exercise either arms or legs, a large wall-rack holding dozens of dumbbells, four fitness benches, something that looked like a rectangular rowboat but not resting in water, a lot of round things on the floor that looked like half-balls with their bottoms cut-off to be flat, and a huge device that looked like it was handed down from a medieval torture chamber. There were also two basketball hoops but they weren't across from each other. The room, of course, was the gymnasium meant only for exercising but, inappropriately, at noon in one of the room's corners was Traci Howe teaching Angus Glass to dance. She was wearing a gray baggy sweat-suit and he was wearing Levis and a white shirt sealed all the way up to the top-button at the neck. Sitting on the hardwood floor was a tall scrawny young man with more hair than he had head and neck and he was wearing a red T-shirt that had a big picture of Mickey Mouse's face sewn on its front and the back of the T-shirt was blue with a big picture of Donald Duck. He was clapping his hands to sustain a rhythm for Angus and Traci who had to be content with the dismal substitution for music that he provided. He had become a human metronome, and seemed proud to be one.

"We need a melody!" Traci almost hollered.

While retaining his duties as a metronome, he started humming something that seemed to have a few different tones so perhaps it could have been thought of as a melody.

President Jared was walking in the hall outside the gymnasium, passed the open doorway and then, on hearing the clapping hands and humming, walked back to the open doorway and yelled out, "Hey, Sinatra! Do you know the words to 'Open the Door, Richard'?"

"No, sir," the man who strived to make a melody said.

"Well, I would expect not. It's an old one. An old ditty. Keep it up, boy. Next thing you know you'll be singing at Carnegie Hall!" And he walked on.

Traci stopped dancing so as not to laugh right in Angus's face.

"What's so funny?" Angus asked.

"Mr. Jared—President Jared. He's so funny!"

"I don't get it."

"Neither do I but that doesn't make any difference."

"Did he say to open the door, Richard?"

"I think so. I guess it's an old song. It doesn't make any difference!"

Now the man who had been a successful metronome and had been complimented by the Acting President of the United States joined in the conversation. "But the door is open. I didn't want to tell him, but it was wide open anyway. So you can't open what's already open. And, hey, you guys were dancing real good. Hey, that was a real blast!"

Traci nodded. "*You* were really doing good, Vahdy! I don't think he even saw Angus and me. He was taken with your talent. Did you hear what he said about you? I'll bet no President of the United States ever told anyone that they'd be singing at Carnegie Hall. I'll bet right now you could be in the Guinness Book of World Records. I'll vouch for the fact that it really happened. Wouldn't you vouch for it, Angus? They need witnesses."

"I'd vouch for the fact that Eli Jared said it, but that won't get Vahdy here in the book of records. Eli Jared is not the President of the United States. He has no title. I don't call him Mister President. Because he isn't. He's Mr. Jared and that's what I call him."

"Aren't you thoughtful, Angus! That will surely win the war."

"All I do is tell the truth."

"You're a silly old toad!" And she backed away from Angus Glass. "I don't want to teach you how to dance anymore."

"Well, a silly old toad—come on."

"Okay, then you're a silly *young* toad."

"You won't think I'm so silly when I'm Vice President under President Desmond."

"Good. Then you can put me in jail."

"I won't put anyone in jail when I become Vice President."

"That's what I'm afraid of. Angus, let's go over to the bikes. People are listening to us here. Vahdy! You want some exercise?"

The three of them walked to the stationary bicycles, and Traci promptly sat on one and started pedaling. Angus sat on the seat of the stationary bicycle next to hers without pedaling, and Vahdy was content to continue standing, this time leaning against the wall.

Angus gripped the handlebars but still didn't even attempt to move his legs as he was too interested in what he was thinking to divert any effort to anything else. "Traci, this is supposed to be the Surviving Executive Branch of the United States, isn't it?"

"Yes. I know what Sebotus stands for."

"But it isn't, is it?"

"What do you mean?"

"Does the Surviving Executive Branch of the United States mean that we make sure we survive and we don't do anything to bring about the end of the killing? What kind of government is this? I don't like it and I wish I wasn't part of it."

She stopped peddling and looked at him sharply. "What is it that you'd do, Angus, if you were in charge?"

"I've thought about it a lot."

"Good."

"A lot."

"Good. What did you come up with? What is the Angus Glass plan for victory?"

"It's not a plan for victory. See? That's what you have wrong. We aren't going to be victorious. We have to have a plan to end the killing."

"And what's your plan for survival without victory?"

"To think in terms of *their* culture; *their* beliefs; *their* hatred of us and understand that it's *our* foreign policy; *our* prejudices; *our* imperialism that causes that hatred of us. They're people too, you know. We have to understand them. If we would understand them we could negotiate and work together to live in peace, not in war as enemies."

"Tell your plan to the President." And she started peddling again.

"I will. I'm going to tell President Desmond."

Now Vahdy displayed an interest in what was being said. He

moved a couple steps forward from the wall. "Hey, friend. What's this President Desmond business? You're going to be Vice President? Wow! Tell me, what's up?"

Traci looked up at him from her bicycle seat. "Vahdy, if you don't treat Angus as a joke, you're even dumber than he is. Angus has found the way to survive!" And she stopped peddling again. "Surrender! Right, Angus?"

"That's the word you use. I use the word 'understand' and I use the word 'culture' and I use the word 'negotiate' and I use the word 'open-mindedness.' And above all I use the word 'peace.'"

"And I use the word 'goodbye.' Find someone else to teach you how to dance. You and your dancing partner can waltz your way outside to those who will chop your heads off when you smile at them while you talk about peace. Do you really think they'll embrace you? They hate you because you're an American. That's why they want to kill everyone I love and that's why they want to kill me. Angus, you're so stupid. I have to go now to wash my hand that touched your hand when we danced. I made the mistake of thinking you were nothing worse than a jerk." And Traci left the bicycle behind and walked out the gymnasium door with her arms swinging by her sides and her hands outstretched, looking as though she was swimming.

Vahdy's eyes opened wide and he shrugged. "Hey, partner—she's mad! Now what's this business with Desmond and you? When are you guys going to take over? What do we have here? Mutiny on the Bounty?"

"Not exactly. I wouldn't call it 'mutiny.' I would call it 'legitimacy.'"

"You're good with words, partner. So what do I do?"

"When we're ready we'll need all the support we can get. Can I count on your support, Vahdy?"

He did not give an answer. "When are you guys going to do it?"

"Oh, there's time. I'm in no hurry. Desmond is in no hurry. You see, nothing is happening here. No one is doing anything. Jared is sitting around in his little world thinking he's president. I got him pegged, Vahdy. And Desmond is the legitimate president. He's on the list of succession."

"Then how did Jared get to be president?"

"He isn't. He conspired with others to make it seem as though Desmond wasn't born in the U.S. which is a requirement of being president. Well, he *was* born in the U.S. And you know something? Even if he *wasn't*, his office is at least on the list of succession. What's Jared? He's nothing."

Less than one half-hour later the man Angus Glass called 'nothing' was receiving an unanticipated guest. Helen ushered the guest in.

"My name is Tchavadar Dey. My friends call me Vahdy. Thank you for seeing me, Mister President." Vahdy was no longer a figure that appeared to be full of adolescent-style fun. He was grim, bold, and noticeably nervous.

"My pleasure. My pleasure. To me, you're Sinatra! How could I say 'no' to Sinatra. Sit down." Eli Jared stood from his desk-chair and extended his hand.

"Thank you, Mister President." They shook hands and he sat down opposite Eli Jared who sat back down behind his desk.

"And I like your shirt."

"Oh, pardon me for that. I came straight from the gymnasium."

"You don't need to apologize. I like Mickey Mouse. That's a good picture of him. When I was a kid my folks subscribed to the '*Mickey Mouse Magazine*' for me. Then the magazine had its title changed to '*Walt Disney's Comics and Stories.*' I loved it. I loved it. And then when I grew up there was a fellow I knew very well named Lyn Nofziger. Ever hear of him?"

"No, sir."

"Lyn Nofziger was a great man in U.S. political life long ago who took policy more seriously than he took himself. A great quality. Not too many people in D.C. had it. Lyn Nofziger always wore Mickey Mouse ties. Every day. He must have had hundreds of them. People bought him all kinds of Mickey Mouse things: ties, coffee cups, watches—Ingersoll watches, badges, all kinds of things."

"No, sir. I didn't know about him."

"Well, it was before your time. But what brings you here, Mr. Dey?"

"Mister President, I don't know whether I'm doing the right thing or the wrong thing, but this is a time when I can't be quiet when something is going on that could ruin everything. This is too important a time to be quiet."

"What do you mean?"

"There is some member of Sebotus—I don't mean the staff but I mean the top Sebotus that—you know, sir—"

"Yes, I know what you mean—a member."

"Yes. He was telling someone else and I was there at the time, and he was saying that we should negotiate with the Islamist revolutionaries—and then he said you aren't really the Acting President; that Secretary Desmond is really the one who should be the Acting President and that he—the one who did the talking—is going to be Vice President under Desmond. It sounded like a plan. He says that you are not doing anything to save the United States."

"I see."

"I'm telling you because I think it can be disruptive for these times. I still think we can win, sir. I don't think it's too late, and I am not prepared to give up or to just let things go."

Eli Jared nodded. "You're a brave man, my friend. And you're right. Thank you for being here."

"I'm telling you all this because he seemed to indicate that he and Desmond have a plan to take over. A kind of a mutiny."

Eli Jared nodded slowly. "I'll take care of it. I'm glad to know; truly glad and I thank you, Mr. Dey. But Desmond is in no shape to do anything. He isn't well. He's a fine man but he isn't well. Dr. Rubins sees him a number of times every day. He doesn't think we have the facilities for him. Secretary Desmond can be alright at—I don't know—alright at two o'clock and not good at all at six o'clock. Dr. Rubins wants him moved but, of course, he knows that's impossible."

"I don't know if this guy is telling me the truth. I believe you should know what I know. I think he can, at least, destroy morale."

"Your appraisal is right. Do you want to tell me his name?"

"No, sir, I don't. I will if you find it necessary to be told but I hope you don't find it necessary to ask me."

"I'm quite sure I know who you're talking about. If it makes you feel any better not to answer, don't say 'yes' or 'no' but I saw who you were with in the gymnasium. If you came straight from the gymnasium to see me, I think I can put that together."

"I was with a lot of people there, sir."

"It wasn't Traci Howe, was it?"

"Oh, no! She isn't anything like that. In fact, she told him off. I thought she'd kill him."

"Good for her. I have no doubt who it is and you don't need to verify it. Mr. Dey, I don't know if it was your attitude when I saw you clapping your hands and making a melody or maybe it was your Mickey Mouse shirt, but out of instinct I knew you were a good man. I'm glad you're here. Carnegie Hall. Isn't that what I said to you?"

For the first time during his visit, Tchavadar Dey gave a smile. "Yes, you did. You said 'you'll be singing at Carnegie Hall.'"

"I'll be in the first row on your opening night, Mr. Dey. And I swear to you, I'll join everyone in the place in standing for you. You're right. It's not too late. We're going to win this thing."

CHAPTER

13

Paper Drives and Victory Gardens

ELI JARED PRESSED the button on his intercom. "Peterson, I find I have some time. I think I'll go kill Angus Glass."

"What?"

"Alright. Alright. Forget that. Just write down how I get to Angus Glass's office and hand me the paper when I walk out the door."

"Wouldn't you rather he come here, Mister President?"

"No. No. I don't see any reason to get blood on our carpet."

His fists were thumping on the door. "Mister Secretary!? Mister Secretary!? Open the blessed door!"

"Who's there?"

"I'm here! Jared! Open the door for God's sake! I've come to kill you."

"To kill me, sir?"

"I have a knife."

There was a long silence from behind the door.

"Well? Well? What are you waiting for?"

"Mr. Jared, are you serious?"

"Now open the blessed door or I'll break it down!"

Angus Glass opened the door cautiously, but there was no caution at all as Eli Jared pushed it in further and stormed into the room with the door practically knocking down Angus Glass. He was able to balance himself and watched Eli Jared walking throughout the room.

"I see you've turned your carefully designed apartment into a freshman's dorm room. It's nice to see those rock-stars looking down at us. Very mature. Very mature."

"Mr. Jared, why are you here?"

"That's right. It's my nickel, isn't it?"

"Yes, sir."

"You know what that phrase means?"

"What phrase?"

"'My nickel.' You know how that phrase started?"

"No, sir."

"It's when pay-phones cost only a nickel for a phone call. It means I called you to tell you something, and it means you didn't call me. Get it?"

"I sort of thought it was something like that. I just never thought about it."

"Well then, since you understand that, I'll let you live a little longer. May I sit down here on top of your guitar?"

"I'll get that off."

"Good. Good. That will make the chair more comfortable for me." Eli Jared didn't wait for Angus Glass's assistance. Instead, he carefully put the guitar on the floor himself and sat down on the cleared chair. "Any last words?"

"Why are you here, sir?"

"Brilliant last words! They can put that on your tombstone. Let me write them down. Got a piece of paper? 'Why are you here, sir?' and then underneath it they can etch the year of your birth and then when I killed you."

"Please, sir. Why are you here?"

"To hear what you have to say to me."

"I beg your pardon?"

"What's going on, Glass? Let's hear it. Do you have anything to tell me?"

Angus Glass thought it over. He dragged a wooden chair to put its back opposite Eli Jared, and then he sat on it backwards, his legs straddling the base of its back. "Okay. I can think of some thing to tell you."

"Go! Quick. Let's go."

"I'm a pacifist."

"That's what you have to say?"

"Well, I think that's bothering you."

"It doesn't bother me in the least as long as you don't try to convert anyone here to your pacifism."

"I'm not trying to convert anyone. But when anyone asks my opinion, they get it. And I think there are better ways than war. I think the way to stop war is not to be a participant in war. It takes two to fight a war."

"It takes only one to kill the innocent. What should we do? Watch?"

"Avoid it in the first place. Don't enact policies that lead others to attack. Our policy should be peace by example."

"I see. It's our fault according to Glass."

"That's right."

"Mr. Glass, you are guilty of visionless morality. Every defeat this nation has suffered was due to a visionless morality of fools."

"Bad policies based on a lack of other people's cultures created hostility against us. Nothing should have been done that would have led others to attack us. Then there would have *been* no wars."

"If only everyone in this nation had always felt the way wise Mr. Glass feels, there would have been no wars! Is that right?"

"That's right. I don't see anything wrong with the United States being a nation of peace."

"Just think! Our Founders could have had peace easily by following the Glass Doctrine. All they had to do was not be Founders. The British wouldn't have gone to war. Keep this territory British. No United States of America. And there would have been peace. President Lincoln could have chosen the Glass Doctrine of peace, settling for two nations; one free, one slave, and he could have saved over one-half million American lives. They would have lived. And there would have been peace. On the Monday morning after December the 7th, President Roosevelt could have invoked the Glass Doctrine, asking the Congress for a declaration of accommodation with what was the Japanese Empire, rather than a declaration of war. And there would have been peace. President Reagan could have ignored Grenada's government, Nicaragua's Sandinistas, and El Salvador's Marxists. The first President Bush, who we call Bush 41 could have said, 'Let Saddam Hussein take Kuwait.' President Clinton could have let Bosnia and Kosovo fall to Slobodan Milosevic. And the second President Bush, Bush 43, could have chosen to accept terrorism as unavoidable. Peace is easy to attain, Mr. Glass. Let the enemy win. Glass, I want unity in this facility. Unity. I don't want anyone around here being a dissenter. Get it?"

"Do you mean you don't want me to give my opinion? You mean my freedom of speech has been violated? Taken away?"

"Now you got it right! Good man, Glass."

"But, Mr. Jared, whether you agree with me or disagree with me, wouldn't you give your life to make sure I retain that right?"

"No. I don't give one hoot about your opinion unless I ask you for it. When I did ask you for it you gave such stupid answers that I don't want you blabbing your protest within this facility unless it's only to me. When there's a war, your rights and my rights and every person's rights are second to the nation's survival. Thomas Jefferson said that 'self-preservation is paramount to all laws.' In peace-time I'd give my life for any ignoramus to state his ignorant opinion, but war puts a temporary hold on that. Get it? A lot of people are killing Americans right now. I do not want the Surviving Executive Branch of the United States to be pacifistic. Therefore keep your pacifism solely to yourself. Clear?"

"But Mr. Jared, then what's the difference between the United States and our enemies? They don't allow opinion that differs with them, and you don't allow opinion that differs with you. Same thing, right?"

"Same thing, wrong. Our enemies don't separate peace from war. We do. During every war in which we've fought for our survival, there were freedoms lost for the duration of the war, some of them unthinkable—or would be unthinkable in peace-time. The list included the closing down of newspapers unfriendly to the war effort; the suspension of habeas corpus; the establishment of relocation camps; the imprisonment of those speaking against our involvement; and the registration, monitoring, and arresting of thousands of aliens. But in every case, after every war was done, our liberties were not only restored, they were increased."

"Like when? Like what?"

"After the Revolutionary War came the U.S. Constitution including its Bill of Rights. The Civil War gave birth to the Emancipation Proclamation as well as the Thirteenth, Fourteenth, and Fifteenth

Amendments to the Constitution codifying the extinction of slavery and requiring the equal protection of the laws.. When World War I was done the Constitution was amended again, this time with the Nineteenth Amendment mandating women's suffrage. After World War II the armed forces of the United States were desegregated."

"And after this war, you say all our liberties will come back?"

"All of them. Plus more. It's always that way."

"I hope you're right. Mr. Jared, if I were president there would be no more wars for the United States."

"I didn't come here to find out what you would do if you were president. I came here to tell you that we have to have unity here, and I don't want you lollygagging around disrupting that unity. Get it? You are Acting Secretary of Housing and Urban Development; in this case a trivial position and even that position may be taken away from you—by me, if I have to, so as to retain that unity. No, I'm not serious when I say I'll kill you but I am serious when I say if you continue to do that I'll lock you up."

"You *do* mean that, don't you?"

"I know what being a wartime president means. During wars for our survival, wartime presidents would have locked you up. So will I."

"Everyone in World War II did whatever Roosevelt wanted?"

"I don't know what was done by everyone but I do remember what was done by such an overwhelming majority that dissent was never an issue. During the projection of newsreels at motion picture theaters, the images of President Roosevelt were always greeted by applause from the audience of democrats and republicans alike. He was our Commander in Chief.

"There was so much unity that every person in the United States was a part of the war effort. No matter their age. I was a little kid in grammar school then, Fairburn Avenue Elementary

School, but the war effort dominated even my time and the time of all my classmates. There were constant paper-drives which meant we would bring a week's worth of newspapers to school to be used for the war effort. And there were what were called scrap drives. We all brought to school any scraps of metal—for the war effort. From empty cigarette packs given to us we would separate the pack's tin foil from its backing-paper and roll the tin foil into a ball and turn it in—for the war effort. My mother saved grease from her frying pan and I brought it to school—for the war effort. I still don't know what was done with that grease, making soap I suppose but I never found out for sure, but everything was based on the war effort.

"Vietnam changed all that. Disunity became the routine. Demonstrations against our policy in D.C. were fun, full of drugs and sex away from home. They were spring breaks with a cause. Fun.

"Then this war—this war—this war came along; a war for our *own* survival; not Vietnam's survival, but *our* survival. Same thing. Fools protested. And even some of the non-dissenters didn't get it.

"Many Americans complained because the price of gasoline had gone up and because we had to remove our shoes before going through security devices at airports. But what a difference from World War II when there were no complaints when gasoline was *rationed*. And there was no taking off shoes at airports—that would have been luxury. Instead the purchase of shoes called for shoe-stamps. The material, when there was any, was synthetic. No complaints. Civilian air-raid wardens were given unprecedented authority during blackouts without facing ACLU lawsuits. No complaints. Cash alone was not enough to purchase most foods and clothes. They were sold with ever-present rationing books and different colored stamps and chips and coupons for meat, for butter, for most groceries. Victory Gardens of vegetables and fruits were grown at home; my mother had a Victory Garden.

"And, I should add, on the battlefields far from home, those in the U.S. Armed Forces fought a totally politically *in*correct war. Good! Had to. We bombed the enemy to blazes. No restraint. Out of it all, we won. And that generation is today justifiably known as what Tom Brokaw called the Greatest Generation. He was right. It *was* the Greatest Generation.

"Admittedly, during World War II, at home there were a number of advantages over this war. First, there was no television back then harping on how terribly the war was going, deflating our morale—and at times we *were* losing. And, thank goodness, there was no United Nations Organization as there was when this war began. If there was a U.N. back in World War II its members would have been writing resolutions until Hitler and Tojo put their flags on American soil just as the Islamist Revolutionaries put their flags on our territory on July the 16th.

"Now the enemy dominates every moment of every life in this nation. It does so because we lost. Our duty here at Sebotus is to try and win back what this nation had. No, Mr. Glass. I will not allow dissent here. I will not allow disunity. You make your choice. Never, never voice one word of disunity except to me alone. If you voice your juvenile, inexperienced opinions to anyone other than me, you will be imprisoned. We do have a prison here and you may well be its first and only inmate. And I mean it. Do you understand?"

"I understand what you're saying, *Mr.* Jared."

"Thank you, Mister Secretary."

CHAPTER

14

Prowee and Prowette

HE WANTED TO be in a more pleasant atmosphere after that encounter and so from the apartment of Angus Glass he walked to the office of Admiral Kaylin without invitation or warning, not that Eli Jared needed an invitation or needed to warn anyone.

"Hello, Joan," he said to Traci, who sat at Admiral Kaylin's outer office desk. "I came here to see Admiral Kaylin. You work for him, Joan?"

She gave that big smile. "Yes, Mister President, I do. But my name is Traci. Traci Howe. You remember that, don't you, Mister President?"

"I called you Joan because I still keep thinking of you as Joan of Arc. But I remember. She was good but she wasn't that good. She wasn't good enough to be Traci of Howe. Isn't that what I told you?"

"That's a good excuse!" she said with a long blink and another wide smile.

"So you work for Keith Kaylin, huh?"

"Mister President, you know that, too!"

"You like him?"

"Of course!"

"I don't like him."

"You don't!?"

"You have to remember that I don't like anyone. No offense."

"Mister President, you just like to startle people, that's all! You don't dislike Admiral Kaylin! You *like* him!"

"I do?"

"Yes. Yes, you do."

"You sure?"

"Yes!"

"I forget things like that."

"Well, you do."

"Ah, so what?"

"Now, do you want to see Admiral Kaylin, Mister President?"

"Not particularly. But since I'm here I might just as well. Is he in?"

"Yes, Mister President."

"Too bad. That's a shame. But you have to take what you get. You might as well tell him I'm here."

"I'm sure you can walk right in, but I'll let him know."

"Wait! What's that thing?" He was looking toward the floor at what appeared to be a black cat with big green eyes and a white triangular marking around its nose and mouth, but it was a stuffed imitation of a cat.

"Oh! That's Prowee."

"Prowee?"

"Yes."

"Is it real?"

"Well, *I* think so."

Then he looked at a chair against the wall with what appeared to be a sleeping tabby-cat. "And who's that?"

"Prowette. It's Prowee's daughter. They're mother and daughter."

"Well, that's nice that they're here. Do they have passes to be here?"

"No."

"How did they get in?"

"They were born here, so they don't need a pass. They're the only ones who don't. Actually, Ollie downstairs in the carpentry shop made them for me."

"I'll bet he did. Maybe he can make me a teddy bear."

She nodded. "I'll ask him if you like."

"Yes. No. I want a cat like you have."

She laughed. "That's good. I'll tell him. Now, may I tell Admiral Kaylin you're coming in to see him?"

"I don't care."

She pressed her intercom button and announced to Admiral Kaylin that President Jared was coming into his office.

Instead of saying "hello" when he walked in, Eli Jared said, "Well, what do you think, Keith?" And he walked directly to a chair opposite Admiral Kaylin's desk and he plopped down on it. "Huh?"

"About what, sir?"

"About Stuart. About what he's doing. About the plan."

"There's no doubt Wayne Stuart is a genius. And he's like you said. He's creative. He's not a businessman or a politician or a military careerist. He's an artist, and he thinks like an artist. He wants to enact a plan—your plan. It might be what we need. As to whether or not it will be effective, or how effective, that's something I can't predict. But no one, including me, seems to have come up with anything else because we have no communications with the

U.S. Strategic Command or with any of our contingency headquarters or—anything. At least it's something. Do you have second thoughts now, Mister President?"

"Oh, no. No second thoughts. I'll tell you what I told him. It isn't going to hurt and, God knows, it might be just what is needed. What I want to know is if you think it will work."

"Mister President, it's a crapshoot."

"Well, who asked *you*?"

Admiral Kaylin gave his short smile. "I think you did, sir."

"That's right. I did."

"Mister President, all I've been doing since this started is trying to think of ideas we can enact without communications."

"That's all you've been doing?"

That one hurt. "Just about. I'm sorry I was late in submitting an idea to you the other morning. I was beat, practically up all night, but I recognize that's no excuse."

"Well, things happen. Things happen. Forgiveness is a known trait of mine," he lied. "Now let's get to today. There are some around here—no names, but there are some who think that what we should do is offer to the revolutionaries some kind of negotiations so our country doesn't get further destroyed. Do you think we can negotiate?"

"I'm a military man, Mister President. I'm not a State Department official who would readily say 'yes, we should negotiate.' My belief is that negotiations with terrorists are better left off the table."

"Mm-hmm. Off the table."

"That's what I believe."

"I asked you because negotiating is a course we could take."

"Then you *are* having second thoughts."

"No. I mean if what Wayne Stuart is doing isn't effective, we have to have a course in waiting. It's derelict if we don't. I believe in the plan we're enacting, but we have to have a backup."

"So negotiate?"

"So *pretend* we're negotiating. Keith, I almost exploded when I heard that anyone here is thinking of negotiations. But it gave me an idea. This is what I'm thinking. I agree with you in totality that you can't negotiate with terrorists. I even come down harder than that. It isn't that you just can't negotiate with terrorists; it's that you can't negotiate with any tyranny. *Any* tyranny. It never works. I also know that the State Department thinks you can negotiate with anyone. I spent a lot of time there. Negotiations are like a religion to State. That's what they're in business to do. So I'm not thinking of negotiating to reach an agreement, but I'm thinking of using negotiations with the Islamist revolutionaries as a decoy—to get some time—to have the clock work a little bit more in our favor; to make them think they're going to get rid of any resistance if they take time to fake a negotiation."

"What good will time do?"

"I'm still holding out the hope that Wadsworth is alive somewhere, and that he's in contact with our military and somehow, *somehow*, maybe he just needs more time. Maybe we can give it to him. Negotiations take time. You can argue about every detail during negotiations. That's a skill of tyrannies. That's what we can do, too. Now, on the other hand it's also true that every moment this goes on is costing lives. I'm living without knowing the facts of what is going on."

"Is there the thought in the back of your mind, Mister President, that maybe we *can* reach an agreement?"

"None. I told you I spent a lot of time with those squares and squishes at State. They have careers based on denying history—denying everything learned in the twentieth century. As far as they're concerned, the twentieth century didn't exist. I used to argue with them all the time. Negotiations in the most prominent disputes of the last century produced nothing but short-range hurrahs and long-range disasters. State doesn't believe it because they don't want to believe it. Nothing to do with facts. Nothing to do with the lineup of twentieth century negotiations starting in 1938 in Munich when Prime Minister Neville Chamberlain signed an agreement with Adolph Hitler, proclaiming the agreement would give peace to Great Britain. 'Peace in our time.' Isn't that what he said? Some peace!

"Then in 1945, President Roosevelt and Prime Minister Churchill accepted the Yalta Agreements with Joseph Stalin of the Soviet Union promising that the countries under Soviet occupation would be given democratic governments, and Soviet domination would quickly end. Lies. Lies. And we signed it.

"Then in 1953 at Panmunjom the U.N. Command under the leadership of the United States began negotiations with North Korea. That was when North Korea was a threat to South Korea alone. A half-century later it became a threat to the world.

"Then in 1972 Leonid Brezhnev of the Soviet Union agreed to an Anti-Ballistic Missile Treaty. The first violation was when the Soviet Union built and deployed a prohibited giant phased array radar station near Krasnoyarsk.

"Then in 1973 North Vietnam signed the Paris Peace Accords promising an end to aggression. Two years and three months after the accords were signed and violated, North Vietnam conquered South Vietnam.

"Then in 1991 the government of Iraq agreed with the U.N. to enforce No-Fly Zones over Iraq, subject to inspection by coalition aircraft. Against the agreement, Iraq consistently fired at the inspecting aircraft they had agreed to accept.

"Then in 1993 the Oslo Accords were signed on the South Lawn of the White House by Yasser Arafat promising Israel peace in exchange for land. Israel gave land and Arafat gave intifadas; violent uprisings and terrorism in exchange.

"Then in 1994 North Korea agreed to freeze its nuclear weapons program. Eight years later North Korean officials admitted they didn't observe the agreement and had produced nuclear weapons.

"Then in 1995 in Dayton, Ohio, Slobodan Milosevic's government of Serbia signed the Dayton Accords to bring an end to the killing in Bosnia. Milosevic simply moved the killing to Kosovo.

"And so, Admiral, not for an instant would I think of negotiating another fraud in the history of negotiations. But as a backup I'm thinking of gaining time. But it calls for certain factors: that our military is putting up resistance; that Wadsworth is alive; that the enemy doesn't know it; that Wadsworth is in contact with the military—and that time will be all he and the military need. That's some gamble, but it's better than opening the doors here with our guns blazing just to go out in glory. Although that's a later option."

"What do you mean?"

"I mean it's a later option. That's why I said it. We have to have a number of courses. One of them, the last one is guns blazing."

"As a military man, that's the option I hate the most, and can plan the best."

"Then put your mind to that one, Keith. I'm going to plan for more middle options."

"Yes, sir."

"Keith, you're a good man. I'm sorry I gave you a hard time the other morning."

"Mister President, I was late in handing in something you wanted. I won't be late again."

"Another good thing about you, Keith. You made a good choice in picking a secretary or assistant out there. She's a nice girl. I forgot her name, but she's a nice girl. I think it's Trudy, isn't it?"

"Traci. Traci Howe."

"Is that it?"

"Yes, sir. Traci Howe. She's a good worker."

Then Eli Jared took the initiative. "A pretty thing, too, isn't she?"

"She is. But she minds her business. She isn't taken with herself."

"She doesn't flaunt it, huh?"

"No, sir. She doesn't."

"That's good. A lot of them flaunt it, you know. Good for her. Well, alright, Keith. I just wanted to run that idea by you and see what you think."

"I appreciate that, sir, and I'll work on plans for the last option you mentioned. I'll do that in the hope we'll never have to use it."

"That's right."

Eli Jared walked into the adjoining office and while the door was still open between the two rooms he turned back to Admiral Kaylin. "Actually, Keith, I came all the way over here to see Trixie, here, not you."

"Traci!" she almost yelled it out, and she had never almost yelled at a president before. "Mister President, my name is Traci!"

He faced her and nodded. "That's right. Of course. But I'm just putting him on, anyway. I didn't really come here to see you. And I didn't come here to see Kaylin, either. I came here to see Prowee and Prowette."

"How come you remember their names and you can't remember mine?"

"They don't talk back like other women."

She laughed. "But they do! Pet them and they meow! Ollie put in a battery thing that makes them meow and purr."

"Even Prowee? Even Prowette?"

"Even Trixie!" she said.

"No. That's not your name."

With a mix of a smile, a look of desperation, and a quick shake of her head, she said, "Mister President, you are, at times, and I mean this with the highest respect both for your office and for you, but Mister President, you are, at times *impossible.*"

"Really?"

"Yes, Mister President."

"I better change."

Traci put her hands to her cheeks as though she was lost in anguish. But then she released her hands, gave that smile with the good teeth and shook her head. "Don't you dare, Mister President. Don't you dare change."

President Jared left her office with the same feeling of inner comfort that he felt many years back when he left Mrs. Zambroski's fifth grade classroom where Suzy Bernard sat in the second seat of the second row.

It was late at night and time for the television monitor to be turned on by Eli Jared within the quiet of his apartment. And, as always, he turned the volume very low.

"Allahu Akhbar! God is Great! This is IFRA's Nightly News of the Islamic Fundamentalist Republic of America. Oh, God, hasten the arrival of Imam al-Mahdi and grant him good health and victory, and make us his followers who attest to his rightfulness." The first scene was in New York showing Fifth Avenue and 50th Street where a sermon was being given by an Imam on the stairway of St. Patrick's Cathedral. The great bronze doors were sealed shut with the announcement made that the interior was being renovated. Then there was a dissolve to the grounds of Fifth Avenue at East 65th Street filled with rubble that had once been Temple Emanu-

El Synagogue. Then a slow-motion videotape was exhibited showing the implosion that caused the bulk of the rubble. The scene then changed to a huge crowd on Third Avenue between 96th and 97th Streets outside the huge copper dome of the New York Mosque, with thousands waiting for the doors of the Mosque to open.

Then it was San Francisco. The screen was showing images of Market Street in San Francisco which was a sea of moving figures in black. Women in chadors were walking between Kearny and Stockton Streets. The videotape shifted to Alta Plaza where a procession of trucks filled with blindfolded men were brought to the center of the plaza and there they were executed so as to be done with as many victims of AIDS as could be shot during daylight hours for public exhibition. An off-screen narrator announced that "by the time August arrives there will be no homosexuals; no homeless; no promiscuity; no depraved in the magnificent city of San Francisco which will become what it was always meant to be.

"Allahu Akhbar!"

Eli Jared turned the television off. "God, please make me forget what I have seen. I have to be a leader. I won't turn on this set again. I should never have ordered it. I don't want to see what I don't need to see. I must appear to be the optimist. I cannot let any of those who work here know that I am a beaten man."

CHAPTER

15

The Letter

THE LETTER HE received was handwritten. Not well handwritten but at least the writer knew how to do it. Even without reading the letter but just looking at it with its handwriting told the addressee that whoever wrote it was old enough to have studied penmanship in school when penmanship was taught. The awkwardness of some of the handwriting was undoubtedly due to one or another ailment that comes to so many with age.

He glanced first at the end of the letter to see who sent it so as to quickly confirm his guess. It was signed, 'Matt' and below that in parenthesis was written, 'Secretary of Commerce, Mathew Desmond.'

And then he went to the beginning of the letter:

Dear Mister President,

I do not want to be a burden to you. I recognize you as the one and only Acting President of the United States of America. I understand that my place of birth is in doubt by some, but it is not in doubt by me. I'm a naturalized citizen. I never lied about that. I was proud of it.

Even if I was born here I would refuse to be Acting President at this time. I am not equipped for the job as it exists today and in all frankness I would not know what to do with that position at this critical time. I do not claim or want a title other than Secretary of Commerce which, at the moment, serves a non-existent function.

I also understand there may be a belief that I was highly medicated in the hospital on the evening of my arrival. The only medication I was given was two Advils. Dr. Rubins told me to take one then and I did, and he said to take the second one if I needed it six hours later. I did not take it. Dr. Rubins wanted to keep me under observation free of extraneous medications. I am confident that he will verify this, as will others on the hospital staff who were there with me that evening. Dr. Rubins was sad and angry that I could not be moved elsewhere with better and more appropriate facilities and—although I hate to say it—with a competent psychiatrist—but the conditions of warfare beyond our walls made it impossible for any movement of me to go elsewhere or for a psychiatrist to come in. The conditions have not changed. Dr. Rubins comes by a number of times every day. He is superb. I would trust him with my life. Anyone would.

I want you to have this letter as an official document. My malady is like a hurricane with bands of intense winds and then quiet and then another band maybe even more intense. Between those bands I have periods of good sense, and so I am taking advantage of this period of good sense to write you this letter. You should have this document.

Mister President, in this country's tradition, we can only have one president at a time. If our elected president is unable to fulfill his duties I am glad that the one president we have is you.

I am your faithful servant and I would be privileged to assist you in any way you want me to assist you, but call on me only if you must. That is not because of any unwillingness on my part, but because of my recognition of my limited and unreliable abilities at this time.

I write this in sound mind.

Respectfully,
Matt
(Secretary of Commerce Mathew Desmond)

CHAPTER

16

The Underground

IT WAS NOT for entertainment but it was the day of the grandest video-game in the history of twenty-first century technology. It was invented by one man in Virginia and set into motion by an international underground of eighty people who spoke thirty-one different languages in thirty-nine countries with one overriding mission: liberty.

The hands of Big Ben in London pointed to 5:02 p.m. (or 17:02 Greenwich Mean Time) and it was 12:02 p.m. EDT as lunch hour had just started at Sebotus Headquarters on Wednesday, July 26.

The time was significant not only in London and in Virginia's Sebotus Headquarters, but was simultaneously significant in other major cities in Europe, the Western Hemisphere, Asia, and Africa where the digital mask of the Virtual World had overtaken the Actual World. It was T-Time.

Skies of blue were being covered with virtual clouds of smoke that were not only frightening but made people cough, not from any change in air quality but a great change in air psychology. There were hundreds of simulated U.S. fighter planes overhead and although there were missiles launched to shoot them down, all of the missile's warheads missed their unyielding targets. Horizons suddenly revealed thousands of fraudulent invading troops and on the farthest horizons were ominous imitations of billowing mushroom clouds sending both civilians and revolutionaries covering their mouths and noses and looking for cover.

And then the Virtual World of illusion was joined by the Actual World of U.S. and allied troops wearing gas-masks that in some cases served no purpose other than the appearance of proper equipment to avoid breathing in toxic gasses or radioactivity, all of which were unreal. And then there were actual attacks and actual bombs and along with them came gas-masks that were not only for appearance but for necessity.

The U.S. and allied troops made prisoners of those with white flags or arms extended and killed those armed adults unwilling to surrender. In city after city, thousands were waving any cloths of white to no more than small numbers of U.S. and allied forces with thousands of fake troops still coming over the horizons, the separation of the real from the imitation remaining beyond any layman's detection.

There were not enough prisons to hold the surrendered revolutionaries and so they were brought to city squares and stadiums as holding grounds, filling them—from Taylor Square in Sydney to Alinamoto Stadium in Tokyo, to Jawaharial Nehru Stadium in New Delhi to Freedom Square in Tblisi, to Teddi Malha Stadium in Jerusalem to Church Square in Pretoria, to Wenceslaz Square in Prague to Plaza de Espana in Madrid, to Twickenham Stadium in London to Estadio Azteca in Mexico City, to Plaza de Mayo in Buenos Aires to hundreds of city squares and stadiums in the United States including RFK Memorial Stadium in Washington, D.C.

On radios throughout the United States the voice of Hashem al-Awadhi suddenly ended in mid-word and there was static and then minutes of absolute silence, then static again, then seconds of silence which was replaced with an unmistakably familiar voice: "My fellow Americans, this is President James Wadsworth."

CHAPTER

17

V-W Day

PRESIDENT WADSWORTH CONTINUED, "I am, this evening, speaking to you on radio from the Oval Office of the White House. Television transmission and reception is not yet able to be put into operation. It is therefore fitting that I start this message by repeating the words of the 33rd President of the United States, Harry S. Truman when he spoke to the American people on what was called V-E Day, Victory in Europe Day, from what was then called the Radio Room of the White House, very close to where I am speaking to you on radio now.

"He said, in part, 'Let us not forget, my fellow Americans, the sorrow and the heartache which today abide in the homes of so many of our neighbors; neighbors whose most priceless possession has been rendered as sacrifices to redeem our liberty.'

"Less than four months later President Truman proclaimed V-J Day, Victory over Japan Day in which he said, 'This is a victory of more than arms alone. This is a victory of liberty over tyranny.'

"Those words of President Harry S. Truman are appropriate this evening, but let me add to them some additional words for this moment. Although this day is a time of monumental victory, it is unavoidably a time to grieve for those whose lives were taken from us, making this generation incomplete for all its years ahead. And even for all of us who are left there is the imprint of such horrors that our very existence will be forever scorched by what we know to have happened. Nothing can be the same as long as we live.

"The list of Americans who have given the ultimate sacrifice is incomplete and we are only now beginning to assemble information. Among those who are gone are many in our government; elected, appointed, civil service and foreign service who have lost their lives in the worst ten days of our nation's history. All the names of all the people gone from all walks of life will forever be memorialized, but that is not good enough. Nothing is good enough.

"There is a great deal to be done and the doing of it must be swift. Lives must be put into as much order as the human mind can muster, communications must be restored, the basics of life have to be accommodated, and fair adjudication must be given to those suspected of the unthinkable.

"We must accurately put together the pieces of how these ten days came about and record all the details of how they came to such an abrupt and victorious conclusion.

"During those ten days, many of the major officers of the executive branch were safe and secure, but through most of that period of time all our communications had been severed by the enemy. We of the elected executive branch had to rely on our armed forces acting alone to deal with the crisis without my coordination or direction. The U.S. Armed Forces performed with magnificence and independence no matter the theater in which they operated. Simultaneously, in a creative and unprecedented act, a previously prescribed U.S. contingency government operated with the most superb and innovative performance, with the most extraordinary and unparalleled leadership that anyone in this nation could have hoped for during this crisis. The full account of those days, including what took place from the contingency headquarters, from our armed forces around the world, and from our allies, will be gathered in a report to the American people and to the peoples of the world. It will be released as soon as all the material can be assembled into one time-lined document. You should know immediately, however, that our contingency government was led by Acting President Eli Jared who I asked to join me tonight but, by his request, will wait until a later time.

"'This moment,' he said to me, 'should be to let the American people know that there is a President of the United States; not an Acting President of the United States, and even more important, that full constitutional rule has been re-established through Executive Order. Please tell the American people,' he said, 'that this is the time to put in order those things that must now be accomplished.'

"Before our full report is able to be released in the days ahead, I am going to follow former Acting President Eli Jared's advice. We will put in order those things that must be put in order and I will meet with those members of the U.S. Congress who have not had their lives taken from their families and from all of us, and those remaining members will assemble quickly to insure that constitutional government is not only restored but is functioning. In addition, state and local governments must be put back in operational order.

"For some time to come I want all Americans to be alert and careful in their reaction to materials that are foreign to them or of unknown origin. It is possible that the enemy has left behind improvised explosive devices of all shapes and sizes. Do not handle unknown objects or even stay in their vicinity. Instead, immediately phone your local headquarters of Homefront Inspection which are being rapidly re-established. Here at the White House we have undergone an extensive sweeping operation today, as are other U.S. federal facilities undergoing sweeps in twenty-four hour days for as long as it takes. This is also true throughout the United States by the remaining local, state, and federal offices of Homefront Inspection. No matter how extensive the inspections, however, caution is mandatory until all areas of concern have been given clearance by the appropriate offices.

"Before this evening is over I, James L. Wadsworth, President of the United States of America, do hereby proclaim this day, July 26 as V-W Day, Victory in the World Day in which our armed forces, the armed forces of our allies, our contingency government, and the undergrounds of our allies regained liberty for this generation of world citizens. As a sign of respect for all those who made the supreme sacrifice during the war that just ended, I have signed a proclamation ordering that the flag of the United States shall be flown at half-staff at the White House and upon all public buildings and grounds, at all military posts and naval stations, and on all naval vessels of the Federal Government, in the District of Columbia and throughout the United States and its Territories and possessions, at all United States embassies, legations, consular offices, and other facilities abroad for a period of sixty days ending on September the 24th, longer than it has ever flown at half-staff in this nation's history.

"This evening will mark the beginning of a new determination on the part of the American people that never again will any generation of Americans be forced to live in fear. Instead, we dedicate ourselves to the conviction that all peoples of our nation and all peoples of the world deserve to live in liberty.

"Liberty is a God-given gift that all people receive at birth, and no government is entitled to steal His gift from those to whom it was given."

CHAPTER

18

Real Rain

ALL THE DOORS and barriers opened for Traci Howe and Admiral Keith Kaylin.

It was the real outside. It was the real sky. There was real earth and real grass and there were real trees and real birds in them and the sun was shining brightly and that was real, too.

"This is how outside looked to me when I was a little girl, when everything in life was new to me and everything outside was thrilling," Traci said softly to Admiral Kaylin. "I went on my hands and knees and felt the grass and then I laid down on my back and looked up at the sky. I remember rubbing my hands on the bark of a tree. I haven't thought about all that again until now. Today, it's the same feeling, only more so because I wasn't thrilled by it for all the years since then. I just accepted it. I don't know if I will ever be able to simply accept it again. Now I think I'll always be thrilled by it. I want to stay thrilled by it."

"I feel the way you do, Traci. The world is a magnificent place."

"It wasn't yesterday."

"Do you want to go for a walk, Traci?"

"Oh, I do. I want us to walk and walk and walk and walk. I want to breathe this air. Where does it all come from? It's so fresh! I hope it doesn't stop."

"It's not going to stop. It's been coming here for millions of years. And it's never stopped." He held her hand and, just as she wanted, they walked and walked and walked and walked.

"Let's go to that tree," and she pointed to a giant oak tree, its branches sprouting out like the thin spokes of an umbrella with thousands of deep green leaves covering the spokes so they were almost invisible, the leaves providing a unified covering making any fabric unnecessary. "Let's sit under it for a moment, Keith."

He nodded. "Let's do that. Now you feel free to call me Keith, don't you?" And as they sat he added, "I lost my rank with you!"

"You're not my boss anymore. And there's no one to hear us."

"I liked you calling me 'Admiral,' but I have to admit that I like it better this way."

"I love saying your name. Now I don't have to salute when I see you!"

"You never saluted!"

"Keith?"

It was too sacred a moment for him to respond by saying "what?" so he didn't say anything.

"Keith—we're free!" And she bent her head back and looked at the view of the sky through the leaves.

For such a learned man he was so inarticulate in this circumstance. It wasn't like war when words of Shakespeare came to him. No Shakespeare now. And no phrases of world leaders or admirals or generals to guide him. But after staring at her as her gaze traveled to take in everything of the outside, he at least chose the *right* words. "I love you, Traci."

In a jolt she stopped her gazing and rested her eyes on him alone. "Do you, Admiral?"

The reprisal of her calling him by his rank was meant to do exactly what it did: confuse him. Somehow, he knew how to handle it. "The Admiral loved you for ten days but he didn't tell you. On the eleventh day, Keith came along and has no hesitancy to tell you." From his back pocket he took out a white handkerchief and gave a few dabs with it above Traci's upper lip. "Your allergy," he explained with a smile.

She was embarrassed. "I'm sorry."

He wasn't. Anything to do with Traci was beautiful.

Later, but still under the tree, the reality of the past and future was seeping into the joy of the current. "Traci, are your folks okay? Did you contact them?"

"Oh, of course I did. I called them from Sebotus the moment we received the all-clear. You know that all of us on the staff of Sebotus had advance word that something was happening that could cause a national emergency. We all contacted our families. Like others on staff, I told my folks to get out of the country and they did. They went to Mexico, just south of Juarez. They're going to head back to El Paso, maybe tomorrow. Do you have anyone, Keith?" She was careful not to itemize any relations or relationships; afraid that maybe, just maybe there was a woman among the ones he cared for.

"Friends. Just friends. My mother and father are both gone. My dad passed away seven years ago. And then my mom just last year. I never had any brothers or sisters, so all I have is friends. I still don't know about them. Most of them are military and a few people who were friends of my folks since I was a little boy. I put all the names on a list and submitted it to the Human Resources Office at Sebotus right after I took the oath there. They extend that courtesy for members. They haven't reported back to me anything through these ten days, but I didn't expect they'd know anything with our communications down. Now I'll find out. Now everyone will find out."

"Keith? How did the war end in such a flash?"

He nodded. "You chose the right word. It was a flash. Or maybe more accurately simultaneous flashes all over the world." And he told her about the ideal collaboration between Eli Jared and Wayne Stuart, and that Stuart had earlier designed and was responsible for the building of the Solarium. He told her about the plan that was devised at Sebotus using augmented reality through a digital mask sent to eighty cities of the world that combined with real troops whose numbers were small but appeared by the enemy to be massive. "You'll learn more later. All the facts will have to be put together but there will be a full report to the public in short time."

"And where was President Wadsworth through all of this? What happened to him through those days? Was he a prisoner?"

"In a sense he was—in the same way that we were prisoners. The enemy made our *own* facilities *our* prisons. This is all unofficial, Traci, so don't repeat it anywhere; wait for the report, but as I understand it early in the morning of the 16th, President Wadsworth and his top staff headed by helicopter to Sebotus Headquarters. But there were too many revolutionaries on the ground near Sebotus. They were visible from Army One, the helicopter, and so they headed off to Andrews Air Force Base. The crisis was growing with such speed that they weren't positive where they wanted to go once they got to Andrews. They tentatively decided on getting aboard one of the Doomsday Planes there. Then, just before boarding, they decided not to do that since they had no idea how long they would need to be in air. They suspected it could be a very long time with in-flight refueling becoming a perfect target for the enemy that's been proven to be proficient in ground to air missile technology. So instead of that, they headed by helicopter to another emergency headquarters near Ansted in West Virginia that was most likely not known by the enemy. It had a cover of not just being a mountain but being a coal mine. There are over 500 coal mines in West Virginia so it seemed they wouldn't suspect the cover that was the headquarters if they suspected any at all. Once the President and the others got in the headquarters, they discovered, like we discovered, that communicating with the armed forces was impossible. Electromagnetic pulse barriers had made all military bases and camps and other facilities free from being contacted by anyone trying to contact them. And there was fear of even attempting to contact another secret headquarters recognizing that the attempt could be intercepted by the enemy and then other headquarters would be revealed. There was no other choice for President Wadsworth and his staff than to just stick it out—like we knew we had to do."

Traci was fascinated with what he was telling her, but when he got to the part about the President going to the headquarters in West Virginia there was the diversion of an occasional rain-drop. Just a few but by the time he said the President and his staff had to stick it out, there were more rain-drops falling than just a few. "It's raining! It's raining!" She put one hand in the earth and sifted through it as rain fell on it making it soft in the wetness. "Look! There's a little spider! I wish I could pet him! But I think he's running because he wants to be sheltered before the rain comes down hard!" And she tried to follow the spider with her hand, her fingers staying close behind it. "I won't hurt you, little spider! I wouldn't think of hurting you!"

"I hope it isn't poisonous!"

The spider ran under some brush. "That one wasn't poisonous.

It's so good to see insects again. I loved seeing them when I was a little girl. I was fascinated with them. Some walked straight and some walked funny. Some had a lot of legs and some didn't seem to have any legs at all. Some could fly. Then, as I grew up, and I don't remember exactly when, but I got scared of them. I'll never be scared of them again. They're little pieces of life. They're living. And they're free! Today we're all free. Oh, Keith; all of us, even that little spider that's hiding is free!"

"Like the spider, do you want to get some shelter?"

"No! I want to stay in the rain. Remember when we saw rain in the Solarium?"

"Of course."

"Oh, how I wanted it to be real rain, but it wasn't. Now it is. Let's get away from the tree! I don't want it to keep us from feeling the rain as it wants to be felt." He stood and bent down to take her hand and she held it tight and propped herself up by gripping his hand, and when she stood she kept her hand as tight around his as when she was rising. They walked as the raindrops fell on them, increasing in intensity and frequency, and soon the rain was pouring on them. But they walked as slowly as they would walk if they were on the sands of a beach on a clear day. "And, besides," she said, "we shouldn't stay under a tree during a storm because there could be lightning. Oh, I hope there's lightning! Lightning and thunder! I love all this! I want it to keep pouring and I don't want any shelter other than you! Will you shelter me?"

It wasn't a difficult request to fulfill. He was an Admiral who was used to much more difficult assignments.

CHAPTER

19

Sailors and Nurses

IT WAS THURSDAY morning on the east coast of the United States and almost every major city center in the world had the appearance of midtown Manhattan after Broadway shows had let out. There were crowds without any sense of destination with people walking to nowhere, shouting in joy, and holding newspapers in their native languages so the short, huge headlines could be seen by others, and almost everyone seemed to have a camera to make a permanent image of their own on a day that would be known in all places for all time to come. All of this took place in cities throughout the world despite the warnings of the possibility of improvised explosive devices left behind by retreating revolutionaries, and despite the ruins of the cities in which they celebrated and despite images ingrained in their heads of what had happened in the seeming eternity of ten days.

And in the real Times Square of the real New York City there were crowds that exceeded its usual New Years Eve except it was day and it was in the summer and there seemed to be hundreds of sailors scattered throughout the crowd all in navy-blue uniforms and there were just as many, or maybe more young women dressed as nurses in white dresses and white stockings. Whether these people were all really sailors and nurses was doubtful, but some of them probably were and they were kissing each other with the sailors and possible-sailors bending the nurses and possible-nurses backward in embrace, in attempted duplication of the 1945 Alfred Eisenstaedt photo whose prominence had endured so many decades as it became a symbol of the end of World War II. But the buildings of Times Square now could not be compared with the buildings of Times Square in 1945, nor could they be compared with the buildings of Times Square less than two weeks back. Some of them were no longer there. Some of their remnants were on the streets. There were yellow tapes everywhere around ruins including the headless statue of George M. Cohan.

In Washington, D.C., Pennsylvania Avenue was closed as a quickly scheduled parade was held with automobile traffic being signaled by police to detour to distances that took the traffic almost to Virginia or Maryland depending on what side of the street the automobiles happened to be heading. Constitution Avenue and Independence Avenue and most of the numbered streets they intersected were also closed as fleets of Homefront Inspection Vans transporting those whose instruments could find improvised explosive devices, and for trucks picking up the already inspected ruins.

The Pennsylvania Avenue parade was scheduled to end after making the bend to 15th Street up to the Treasury Building and to stop there rather than making the turn of the Avenue to go as far northwest as the White House, but that didn't stop huge crowds from gathering outside the White House filling the Avenue and filling Lafayette Park across the street and all the adjoining streets. Unlike so many demonstrations in front of the White House through the pre-war years, many of the people held banners saying, "Thank God You're Safe, Mr. President" and "Wadsworth Forever!" and "Victory!" and "We Won!" and "U.S.A." and "It's Over, Over Here!"

President Wadsworth was in the quiet of the White House's Oval Office sitting on his yellow lounge chair facing Eli Jared who had his black eye-patch placed over his left eye and he was sitting on another yellow chair and so was Wayne Stuart who was in a place he had never been, and appropriately though uncharacteristically he was wearing a black suit and red tie, and was very self-conscious about his long and full hair that he did not have an opportunity to have cut for this meeting.

The appearance of the Oval Office was remarkably the same as it had always been. It looked as though the invaders intentionally did little damage to it or whatever damage that might have been done had been removed and pre-invasion appearances were quickly restored in the day since victory. The flag of the United States and the flag of the presidency and the flags of the U.S. Armed Forces had made a return appearance. At least on the surface, the Oval Office looked as it had looked during the normal days of the Wadsworth Administration.

President Wadsworth, very characteristically, was at least attempting to look at ease on that yellow lounge chair, his legs crossed and smoking a cigarette. "Let me give you the schedule. As you know, full constitutional law has been restored just as you wrote on your Executive Order, Eli. I re-executed it last night. The restoration of all monuments, memorials, shrines, and national properties will be underway in full next Monday with some of them starting today. I am calling for tomorrow, Friday, to be a Day of Prayer for those taken from us and a day of thanksgiving that the enemy has been defeated.

"Eli, tomorrow night I want you to make a speech to a Joint Session of the Congress. It was a decision that was unanimously endorsed by the members of the Congress that we could contact. Mr. Stuart, because of the high recommendation of Mr. Jared, on Saturday morning at ten o'clock here in the Oval Office I am making a presentation to you. It's the Medal of Freedom. That, Mr. Stuart, is the highest civilian award a president can bestow on anyone."

"Thank you, sir."

"You should know that was the first recommendation President Jared gave me."

Wayne Stuart turned to face Eli Jared. "Thank you." And then he turned to President Wadsworth. "Thank you."

President Wadsworth nodded. "You are so welcome, Mr. Stuart." He turned his head to Eli Jared. "Also Eli, as you recommended, I will give the Distinguished Service Medal to Secretary Desmond and to Admiral Keith Kaylin. Now, I am positive that some committee of the Congress or any number of committees will ask for a report on what happened during those ten days the Surviving Executive Branch of the United States was in operation and you might designate some of your people to start working on that. In fact, you might as well have them make it a report for me at my request, and then you will have all the material for the Congress when their committees ask for the same kind of thing. The only difference between them and me is that they will probably ask you questions for days and days. I only have praise.

"Mr. Stuart, I have a couple of souvenirs for you, that is if they have been replenished this morning. Let us see," and he walked to his desk and opened its top left-side drawer. Then he nodded. "Here is a tie-clasp for you. It has the presidential seal and all that—and some cuff links—and something else, and this one I know is here." He walked to the white shelves that held knick-knacks and a few books. He took one book off the shelf. "The inspection team found this book here this morning. It's in Arabic. You can tell your grandchildren that this book was left behind in the Oval Office by the enemies of the United States some time during the ten days of their take-over and given to you by the President of the United States the day after victory—the victory you did so much to bring about."

Wayne Stuart shook his head and said the now-familiar "thank you" that he had said so many times during this visit.

"Mister President," Eli Jared asked, "how were you able to put together such intense inspections throughout the nation with so many vacancies in the bureaucracy to do the work, and probably thousands who have yet to get in touch with their own departments and agencies?"

"What was it Kennedy said? When the going gets tough, the tough get going. Also, there is the unsaid rule of government: The smaller the bureaucracy, the more you can achieve."

Eli Jared nodded. "No. You certainly can't say that publicly but I know what you're saying is true." And Eli Jared took a big brown cigar from his suit-jacket pocket. And there was the President of the United States lighting it for him. Eli Jared continued, "I remember the most successful days of NASA were when it was just starting. That's when it had no bureaucracy. None. Its headquarters were small enough to be located in the Dolley Madison House on 'H' Street across from Lafayette Square where Dolley Madison lived after President Madison died. Just up the street from here. I think it had about twelve people working there. God, what they did! Remember that, Mister President?"

He nodded with a smile. "I do. Eli, can you stick around for a while? I know you probably want to get to writing your speech for tomorrow night, but if you can, let's have a bite and talk."

"Of course, Mister President. I'd like that. Frankly, I would like to hear what you've been through while I've been hiding at Sebotus!"

"And I want to hear what you have been doing for the past ten days in that little facility of yours in Virginia! Isn't it something? For as long as our generations last, no matter where they were, people will be talking about what they went through and asking their friends what they went through. Almost everyone in the United States and in so much of the world went through what we all thought humans could not endure—some of them didn't—but some like us, are fortunate enough to be able to talk about it. Or maybe it isn't so fortunate for us. All of us are wounded, some deeper than others, but all of us are wounded . . . severely." He paused and there is nothing more silent than the Oval Office when no one is saying anything.

CHAPTER

20

Joint Session

IT WAS 9:00 p.m. in Washington, D.C. on Friday, July 28, and the chamber of the House of Representatives had an audience of senators and representatives and the Supreme Court and members of the President's cabinet. Beyond the chamber, television viewers throughout the nation and viewers of other nations throughout the world were watching.

There were any number of vacant seats in the chamber. That was not normal for a Joint Session of the Congress. The abnormality was defined by bouquets of flowers placed on vacant seats. The front of the chamber looked almost the same as it did before July the 16th when the horror began. The flag of the United States had been quickly hung behind the Speaker's chair as it used to be and the only visible changes toward the area of the rostrum were the empty frames that used to house the painting of George Washington and the painting of Lafayette on the wall to the left and to the right of the rostrum. The Islamist fundamentalists had cut the paintings to shreds and so, today, the hanging shreds had been taken down, while the empty frames remained to border copies of the originals on a later day if the shreds could not be rejoined.

At President Wadsworth's request the doorkeeper entered the door at the rear of the chamber and yelled, "Mister Speaker, the Former Acting President of the United States!"

The audience of the chamber rose and applauded and cheered and the ones by the aisle extended their hands to Eli Jared as he walked from the rear to the front of the chamber. He nodded from side to side and shook some hands but not many and the applause and cheers went on as he made his journey to the podium. And the applause and cheers went beyond his journey.

As he stood there, the Vice President and the Speaker of the House, standing on the rostrum behind him kept applauding with the assemblage. Then the Speaker of the House banged his gavel over and over again and slowly the applause faded as the assemblage sat.

The Speaker of the House shouted, "Members of the Congress, at the request of the President of the United States I have the high privilege and distinct honor of presenting to you the former Acting President of the United States."

And again the standing ovation, and again the gavel and again the dying down of the applause. They sat as Eli Jared spoke:

"Mr. Speaker, Mr. Vice President, members of the House of Representatives and the Senate, honored guests, my fellow Americans and people of the world, please accept my appreciation for your attendance and the welcome you have given me. Just as President Lyndon Baines Johnson said when he stood on this very spot on November 27 of 1963, 'All I have I would have given gladly not to be standing here today,' I, too, would give gladly all I have, not to be standing here this evening. President Johnson was referring to the assassination of President Kennedy that cast him, as Vice President, into the role of the presidency. I refer to the horror of the war that cast me as nothing more than a private citizen into a role none of us would seek under the circumstances of July the 16th.

"Since that date most of the people of the world have lived through the unlivable. And so an even more difficult task than the victory we attained awaits us: Never again!

"Ahh, but that's what was said in the 1940s about the Holocaust, wasn't it? And also in the 1940s we said "Remember Pearl Harbor" didn't we? And that's what we said in the 1970s about the genocide of Cambodia, isn't it? And that's what we said in 2001 about 9-11, isn't it?

"On that date even skeptics realized we were in a war against those who wanted us killed and our nation killed and even themselves killed in the doing of it, all for imagined rewards to be given in the after-life for their killing. And we all knew that preemption on our part would be vital. But soon the realization faded and so did the unity. Complacency was reflected in polls that tabulated that the chief concern of Americans was the economy. And then health care. And then the environment. And further down the list was terrorism. After all, 9-11 was quickly considered to be history, not the current. Therefore, *unity* was history, not the current.

"We, characteristically, find anything in the past to be a long time ago. Americans are a uniquely impatient people. We are a people who buy Sunday newspapers on Saturday, we buy April magazines in March, next year's models of cars are out this year, and we rush to the future as we receive Christmas catalogues in September. We are the authors of fast food. Our inherent American impatience is a great asset in peace-time but it can mean defeat in times of war.

"I make these points to you tonight because we didn't remember, or more likely we ignored what we knew. We could have avoided *this* war decades back if we remembered, or if we didn't ignore what we knew to be true, and there would have been no empty seats around the television sets across the nation this evening—or empty seats in this chamber tonight. As this war started we took comfort in knowing that every Chief of State around the world knew that we had more power than any other nation in the world, and that our military had the means to destroy any enemy, and destroy any enemy in short time. But what we didn't realize was that because of Vietnam in 1975, Lebanon in 1983 and Somalia in 1993, the world had come to believe we wouldn't use the power we had, and therefore we were *not* the most powerful nation in the world. And that is crucial because the victor in any war is not necessarily the one who has the most power—it is the one that is perceived as willing to use the power that will achieve its victory.

"And even after some 3,000 civilian lives were lost on 9-11 our troops were ordered to fight a politically correct war on the battlefields, and we fought a politically-correct war at home as well, advocating peace-time rules to apply in war. We let it be known that the enemy could win if it was patient enough and cruel enough. How then, could we avoid what we went through this month? We couldn't. Almost with pride, we had proclaimed our impotency.

"And so, in the end we had to do what we should have done in the beginning. And at the end there was little with which to do it. But we did it with what we had, and we won.

"We must never be brought to the brink again. Never again 'peace dividends' to reduce our defenses in the illusion that there are no more enemies on the horizon. Never again complaints about domestic profiling during wartime. Never again the outrageous political announcement that 'I support the troops but oppose their mission.' No issue of diversion from winning the war. Not insistence of government provided health care or environmental issues or lower costs for prescription drugs or a host of social issues. All of those topics should be nothing more than luxury for a later time so that they are not decided by foreign conquerors. Generations prior to ours put victory first and did things they didn't like to do so that future generations including our own could inherit the liberties we had—but were too often misused. And I must add, never again a need for an *acting* president. Always a November-*elected* president.

"But, realistically, this month will likely be forgotten or ignored in short time. Even in this chamber the horror of this month will likely be forgotten or ignored by some members in favor of the quest for more personally rewarding issues, encouraging those things that guarantee their reelection rather than warning their constituents of what lays beyond the horizon should we fail to act. And so what happened this month will likely happen again if history can serve as a prophet.

"Some in this chamber never sought to win this war. Hell was not perceived as a distant defeat for the nation but a quicker defeat for themselves; a fear of losing their public stature; of being insignificant in their district, of being unimportant in the eyes of their peers; of being treated with indifference and to be unrecognized by strangers.

"The only war they were equipped to fight was a war to retain their own power.

"Even now, to some in this chamber, God, Himself, is perceived as a competitor."

And Eli Jared left the podium. There was no grand ovation. Only a few stood and applauded.

CHAPTER

21

Protest

THIS TIME WASHINGTON D.C.'s Pennsylvania Avenue was not closed for a celebration, but for a demonstration. It was scheduled to start at twelve-noon with the march starting on Capitol Hill and ending across the street from the White House in Lafayette Square.

By the time the first marchers who were holding upside-down U.S. flags reached the avenue's intersection with Ninth Street, the student-marchers behind them packed the heart of the avenue including the sidewalks and they appeared to be one big slow-moving mass holding banners expressing their protest: "Who Elected Eli Jared?" "No More U.S. Nukes!" "U.S. Out of Everywhere." "Wadsworth—Pawn of Jared." "How Many Nukes Did You Use?" "No More Wars!" "It's a Globe, Not an Empire." "No More Money for Killing!" "U.S. Imperialism!" "Jared and Wadsworth = Hitler and Hitler." And there were smaller banners saying "The Answer is the Answer Coalition." Mixed in with those holding banners were others who were holding placards, some of them with a big diagonal slash on a red circle over the names of Wadsworth and Jared and other placards with pictures of Presidents Wadsworth and Jared with circular targets on their chests and "Impeach Wadsworth. Convict Jared" written beneath the pictures.

For seemingly no reason at all some of the demonstrators started beating at the doors of the Justice Department until the police came and escorted them back to the sidewalk and street and then demonstrators started doing the same thing to the Old Post Office Building and this time the police arrested maybe a dozen of them, taking them to police busses lined on 12th Street.

The demonstration was restored to some kind of order, with the demonstrators resorting to yelling a statement with question and answer chants:

"Impeach Wadsworth!"

"When do we want him impeached?"

"Now!"

"Convict Jared!"

"When do we want him convicted?"

"Yesterday!"

They kept it up as they made the turn north up 15th Street where Pennsylvania came to its temporary halt, then they turned left to where the rest of Pennsylvania Avenue continued toward the White House.

When they arrived near East Executive Avenue to the margin of the White House compound, the chants became louder with the demonstrators behind the first rows starting to push the people up front so they would move faster, then everyone behind them seemed to push the people ahead of them, the demonstration turning quickly into a near-riot. Some tried to get to the White House fence.

It didn't last long. Lafayette Park, across the street from the White House, was not an empty park waiting for demonstrators. For hours it had been filled with waiting police who now formed themselves into a human wall coming toward them. The demonstrators started throwing stones at the police and yelling obscenities at them preceded by the call of "Wadsworth's Storm Troopers!"

After one policeman was felled by a rock that hit its target, the police became more than a human wall, bathing the demonstrators in tear-gas. They ran away from the police in all directions and went throughout the city, turning D.C. into a city of anarchy.

What saved the District of Columbia was an afternoon thundershower. Demonstrators traditionally despise rain, and these demonstrators were no exception.

That night when the rain was done, they congregated in West Potomac Park where television reporters went from one demonstrator to another for interviews for their evening newscasts. There was no shortage of those who wanted to give their words of protest on television but it became quickly apparent to the interviewers that the interviewees were very young and not able to articulate why they were there. Some of them, both boys and girls, were able to cry when they talked about what they called U.S. imperialism. Outside of that, the television newscasts concentrated on earlier tapes of the demonstration as a whole, rather than individuals.

The obvious question was 'why are you here today?' The answer became apparent only after the television crews left. That was when West Potomac Park became a giant bed with sleeping-bags filled with two or more people in them. The tear-gas that permeated the air earlier was now replaced with an acrid odor that, other than to the ones who created it, was not even as tolerable as the earlier sharpness of the tear-gas.

It didn't take long for much of the nation to readjust itself back to the joys, the goodness, and the faults of what was normality.

CHAPTER

22

Executive Privilege

GEORGE CUTLER WAS the counsel to the President and was rarely in the Oval Office, but he was called to be there by President Wadsworth after the President read a memo George Cutler had sent him. In the memo George Cutler told the President that a Senate-Select Committee was going to be assembled to investigate all activities that took place at Sebotus Headquarters during the ten days of crisis. There was no question that this was not going to be a friendly gathering of supportive senators.

President Wadsworth had come back into familiar territory: the determination of the political opposition. "Where's Eli? Where's Jared? I want him to come here."

George Cutler, who sat opposite the President, shook his head. "We tried to get hold of him this morning, Mister President," George Cutler answered without answering. "He can't be reached. Every day he goes to visit victims of the war, going from one hospital to another in D.C., Maryland, Virginia, the whole area. He doesn't leave word on how to get hold of him because he obviously doesn't want to be interrupted. My office left word that I want him to call me, and at the same time we asked the Bureau to send out some locators. So we or they should get hold of him soon or we'll just wait to hear from him whenever he gets home and listens to his answering service or answering machine or whatever primitive device he has. That is, if he ever gets in the mood to listen to his messages."

"That's Eli. Visiting hospitals. Look, George, we cannot let the Senate make a circus out of all this and take advantage of demonstrations in the streets against Jared and against me. With this congress you can just imagine who will be appointed to be on a Senate-Select Committee on the Surviving Executive Branch of the United States. Can you imagine? They will find some supercilious witnesses and get what they want out of them. You can be sure they will attempt to make Jared and this administration out to be the villains of the nation."

"Of course. The talk is that Donald Simmons will be Chairman of the committee."

"Oh, for Pete's sake! That fellow is as arrogant, pompous, and self-centered as anyone who ever strutted on Capitol Hill. He will try to push a sword into Jared and he will take it out and dig it into us. What we have to do is—no question—invoke Executive Privilege."

"I assumed that's what you'd want to do. But we'll have trouble with it."

"Why?"

"Because presidents have always had trouble with it ever since the first president started asserting it."

"Who was the first president to use it?"

"The first president of the United States, George Washington. But he had trouble with it and after him they've all had trouble with it."

"Brief me on it, George. But a quick one. Thank goodness I have never had reason to use it before."

"The main problem is that it isn't in the Constitution. But—but implicit in the Constitution is the separation of powers between the branches of government. As you know, the first three articles of the Constitution clearly separate the duties and responsibilities of the three branches of government, and so Executive Privilege has been used to maintain that separation. Other than in some special cases, the Supreme Court has gone along with that reasoning."

President Wadsworth got up from his desk and paced near the window overlooking the South Lawn and beyond to the Ellipse and the Washington Monument and the Jefferson Memorial. "Then let us go ahead and take whatever the Congress throws at us. We are certainly entitled to have confidential discussions with our advisors and not have them hauled out in some public spectacle while senators demand they tell the world what they advised and what our private conversations were all about."

"You don't have to convince me, Mister President," George Cutler said. "But beyond the problems they'll throw at you, we might have some unique problems that past presidents haven't had."

"Why? What?"

"Eli Jared was an acting president and he had no staff as such. He didn't have the staff members as we know them in the West Wing and the Eisenhower Executive Office Building. His acting cabinet became his staff. That's unusual. They might say cabinet officers always have to testify to the Congress for oversight of their own departments. I think it's a non-starter because cabinet officers don't have to testify about private conversations with the president so why should they now? But they're sure to make something of it. The more points they make, valid or invalid, the more public opinion gets muddled. Our position should be that beyond a doubt it was the only staff the President had and he needed candor and the legislative branch has no business grilling them on what they said and he said. Doing so would interfere with the separation of powers. That's all. Keep it simple and don't bring up all kinds of things that have no bearing."

"Can I do this for a former president—and a former *acting* president at that? I mean, can I establish Executive Privilege for the actions of another president? How about if it isn't me who establishes Executive Privilege right now but Jared does for the period he served? Can Jared assert Executive Privilege?"

"At this stage, I'm sure he can't, although this has never come up before in our nation's history. My best guess is that you, as president, would have to assert it—invoke it on his behalf, and really on your own behalf. It's a different man but it's the same administration. You appointed him and you appointed his acting cabinet to represent you. That's sound. After all, the idea is to retain the precedent used by George Washington forward. There shouldn't be an exclusion made for periods in which there are acting presidents."

"Do you think we can win on this?"

George Cutler nodded. "I do. But you should be aware of the mess this will bring about. And you also don't know if there are some who worked for Jared in that facility who might seek a moment of public glory by not obeying your Executive Privilege and testify anyway. There'll be television cameras and all that. With that kind of temptation, you can't count on 100 percent loyalty and neither can Jared. There's at least one public-spotlight-seeker in every administration. Every president should count on it."

President Wadsworth went back to his desk and sat down behind it. He revolved in his chair to look at the inspirational view beyond the South Lawn, and then he turned back to George Cutler. "You know what Eli once told me?"

"What?"

"'Cameras are to some men what beautiful women are to others: irresistible! There is something wrong with their genes.'"

"He has a point!"

"Who on the committee do you think will be on our side?"

"No telling. But the *other* side will have the Chairman and they'll have the majority of the senators. It's a Senate-Select Committee, not a regular committee so we can't predict names. We won't be without support. And maybe there will be a few surprises like one of our guys turning on us and supporting them and one of their guys supporting us. It happens."

"Jared has got to be in on this. No matter how much I would like to just go ahead and do it, it isn't a decision I should make alone since it involves him to a higher degree than it involves me. Courtesy alone dictates we let him have his say on this. Frankly, it demands that we let him not only have his say but let him have his way on this. Try him again, George."

George Cutler nodded and took his phone from his pocket, punched the numbers, and waited. "No soap. No answer. Just his service. No need for me to leave another message. He already has one from me. And we have our locators looking for him."

As soon as he put his phone back in his pocket the intercom on President Wadsworth's desk buzzed. He put the desk phone to his ear. "Yes . . . You what?" And he put the intercom on speaker and put down the phone. "Repeat that, Marianne."

"We have word on Eli Jared."

"Do you have him on the line?"

"No, Mister President. He's at George Washington University Hospital."

"Good! Yes, we knew he was visiting victims of the war."

"No, he's not visiting anyone there."

President Wadsworth was silent. And very slowly he asked, "Then what is he doing there, Marianne?"

"He's a patient. He's fine, Mister President. He's doing just fine. He had chest pains but he's doing fine. Nothing critical. I'll get to that in a moment but he gave orders that no one be notified he's in the hospital, and you know Mr. Jared when he gives orders. It was our Bureau people who were able to locate him. He gave orders to them not even to tell you. But, as you can tell, they disobeyed him since he isn't president anymore and you are. They won't tell anyone beyond telling me to tell you."

"That is not the issue. What did they say about his condition?"

"I'm getting to that, sir. Good. They say he's fine. He's not in I.C.U. or listed as critical or serious or anything like that."

"Is that information you were told from the doctors, and not from him?"

"Yes. I was told by a Dr. Kelo there, that Mr. Jared has been given an extensive series of examinations and he has more scheduled but he and the other doctors think he's going to be just fine and, more than anything else, they say he needs rest. Rest, treatment and observation is the way Dr. Kelo put it. He said that Mr. Jared is being his usual cantankerous self. Apparently he didn't like the diet they ordered for him from the hospital kitchen and he threw some Jell-O on the floor—intentionally."

"Jell-O! Who could get that mad at Jell-O?"

She knowledgably answered, "Mr. Jared."

"Good for him!"

President Wadsworth turned off the speaker and looked at George Cutler. "Life takes incredible turns, George. I have learned it so many times. For good and sometimes for ill, life takes incredible turns. To be prepared for all of them is simply beyond our capabilities."

CHAPTER

23

The Hearings

THERE WAS A large crowd outside the bronze doors of the north entrance to the Dirksen Senate Office Building. Everyone in the crowd was waiting to get further up in the slow moving line going through security before getting to Senate Committee Room 226. The line included reporters, still photographers, television cameramen, and there were members of the government, and some from the general public, and they were all there to see the committee's single witness for the day: former Acting Secretary and current Assistant Secretary of Housing and Urban Development, Angus Glass.

All the commotion and crowds and security caused the hearings to be delayed forty-five minutes beyond the scheduled beginning of the session that had been planned for 10:00 a.m. The gavel finally sounded and the Chairman of the Senate-Select Committee on the Surviving Executive Branch of the United States, Senator Donald

Simmons called the Hearing Room to order and he went through the customary formalities. He then welcomed the witness, telling Assistant Secretary Glass how courageous and patriotic he was to "be here without protest" in cooperation with the committee and agreeing to testify even though the President had invoked Executive Privilege to prevent such testimony.

After the Chairman's lauding of Angus Glass's courage and patriotism, Chairman Simmons asked him, "Assistant Secretary Glass, would you rise, please?"

A very nervous Angus Glass stood up. He always looked nervous under the most normal circumstances but this time there was some excuse for his nervousness as he stood before the Chairman and seventeen other sitting senators who faced him at their greatly elevated quarter-moon shaped rostrum. Angus Glass was looking at them as he stood in front of the chair provided for him at a green-clothed table accompanied by three lawyers on the chairs to his sides. Added to all of that, he was well aware there was a large audience sitting behind him and beyond all that were millions of viewers and listeners throughout the country watching and hearing it all on television.

The Chairman cleared his throat and asked, "Do you solemnly swear that the testimony you will present before this Senate-Select Committee will be the truth, the whole truth, and nothing but the truth, so help you God?"

"Yes, Sir, Mr. Chairman."

"You may be seated."

Angus Glass looked uneasily to either side with a slight and hesitant smile and sat down in front of the desk microphone facing him.

Chairman Simmons continued, "Assistant Secretary Glass, we welcome you here for this most important oversight hearing. We note some of your recent comments showing your great concern over your experiences at what is called Sebotus Headquarters during the recent crisis that befell the nation so critically. Your comments have been described in many media in the last number of days and your forthrightness has received the attention of our committee. We welcome your willingness to testify and I want you to know that we are gratefully aware of the hardship placed on you due to the general attitude of the White House regarding these procedures. We look forward to your testimony.

"Do you have an Opening Statement?" he asked although the Chairman already knew that Angus Glass had an opening statement because the Chairman had a transcript of it in front of him as well as knowing that copies had already been placed in front of the seventeen other senators seated at the rostrum.

"Yes, Mister Chairman," Angus Glass answered and he started reading. "I would like to make an opening statement to the distinguished members of this Senate-Select Committee."

"The floor is yours."

"Thank you, Mister Chairman," he ad-libbed at the unexpected four-word interruption and then he went back to his reading. "Following the attacks of July the 16th I reported to the headquarters of the Surviving Executive Branch of the United States, referred to here as Sebotus. I was expected to report there in case of a declared national emergency. That contingency assignment was relayed to me by the Secretary of Housing and Urban Development under the direction of the President of the United States shortly after I became Assistant Secretary of Housing and Urban Development. On July the 16th when I heard of the emergency I immediately went to the Pentagon where I was taken by helicopter to Sebotus Headquarters in Virginia. As previously agreed, I will be glad to give the exact location in closed hearings."

Angus Glass then went on to give an oral tour of the Sebotus facilities in a successful attempt to dazzle the senators with his knowledge of the place they had never seen and had no familiarity of it prior to the last few days of leaked reports in the media. Then he got to the heart of his prepared testimony that went beyond dazzling:

"These facts in my following testimony are not easy for me to expose but I find I must because they were in such contradiction to anything I would have expected of the country I love, and whose freedoms were guaranteed by our most sacred documents, the Declaration of Independence and the Constitution of the United States." The lawyer to his immediate left who was very fat and had a large horizontally-shaped face, nodded in brisk motions with his two lips joined tightly as one, signifying he had probably written that sentence.

"There was only one person present at Sebotus Headquarters who was part of the line of succession to the Presidency. That was Secretary of Commerce Matthew Desmond. The night he arrived, both Eli Jared and Admiral Keith Kaylin hurriedly met with him. I had been present and alone with Mr. Jared when the announcement was made that Secretary Desmond was on the premises. It did not seem to me that Mr. Jared was particularly glad when he heard that announcement, although I do not recall his precise words. I do remember that Mr. Jared quickly interrupted our meeting to get to the Secretary. As I understand it, instead of taking directives from Secretary Desmond, Mr. Jared and Admiral Kaylin brought him to the Sebotus Hospital where he stayed overnight. I do not know what went on there but I do know the following morning the members of Sebotus and some of the top staff attended a meeting in which we were all given our assignments. Secretary Desmond had entered the meeting looking dazed and he was supported on the arm of Admiral Keith Kaylin. The assignments were announced and that was when I was about to be told that I was named on the President's list to be Acting Secretary of Housing and Urban Development. The meeting had been turned over to Secretary Desmond who appeared to be under the influence of either a narcotic or something of which I am not aware. He also appeared to be frightened. He immediately announced that he had been born in Hamilton, Bermuda of British parents and then we were told that since he was not born in the United States, he could not be Acting President of the United States. This was accepted by the participants at the table although no one examined any credentials if there were any. It was then announced that President Wadsworth had ordered that should no one be present in the line of succession, Eli Jared was his appointed Acting President of the United States. Remember that Eli Jared was not even a current member of the United States Government. I am not suggesting that this was not legal, but it was a surprising appointment.

"In my view, Mr. Jared then ran events, not as Acting President but more like an acting dictator, and I give the following as evidence and backup to my claim:

"Before enacting his secret plans—his grand design—he never consulted with the cabinet members. As example, I had no idea what was going on.

"When seven others tried to get onto the facility grounds he had them killed by allowing, and I believe directing Admiral Kaylin, to flick a button that collapsed the earth under them and bury them. The earth swallowed them up and I am sure their bodies—their corpses—all of them, seven of them—are still underground. No taking of prisoners, no trials; their deaths simply ordered by Eli Jared. When I asked him if Acting Attorney General Jonathan Hynd had been consulted or even notified, he responded proudly that he never told the Attorney General.

"When I mentioned to him the importance of the Geneva Conventions and the treatment of the enemy mandated by the Geneva Conventions, he belittled those international agreements and proceeded to give me a speech in which Mr. Jared belittled HUD, the Department of Housing and Urban Development. As if to emphasize his authority, I was never given an assistant or even a secretary for the entire time of the crisis although there were any number of assistants and secretaries available.

"He went on to threaten that he would put me in shackles and even made remarks about executing me. Perhaps he meant that part as a joke but it was not very funny, particularly in light of the executions he had ordered of the seven men who had come to the exterior of the headquarters and, as I said, whose bodies are still in the ground there. This was, in my view, the orders of a dictator, not an Acting President of the United States of America.

"Mr. Jared also lectured me on the value of war, going through a list of wars whose deaths and destruction he totally ignored. He seemed to take particular delight in war. He knew, full well, and said so, that I was a philosophical pacifist.

"He was a very frightening figure. I believe I am fortunate—and it was pure luck—to have survived those ten days.

"For the purpose of brevity I am leaving a number of events and a number of details out of this summary but, at request, I would be glad to fill in anything the Chairman or distinguished senators would like to know.

"I am testifying, Mister Chairman, in the hope that other witnesses will come forward. If they will, I believe my statements will be verified and, perhaps, filled in by others who witnessed things I did not see. I hope they will testify, but if this table for witnesses is any indication, then I am not encouraged. There seems to be an invisibility of other witnesses here.

"That, too, is brought about by the dictatorship, as I would call it, that overrode the Constitution during those ten days and has spread even to these days although the crisis is over. Executive Privilege is the excuse and justification given by Eli Jared and now by President Wadsworth to keep the workings of the executive beyond your knowledge and beyond the knowledge of the people of the United States.

"Finally, Mr. Chairman, I have disregarded Executive Privilege and my order to obey it because of my belief in the Declaration of Independence and the Constitution of the United States as I stated to you earlier, and also because of my belief in the Geneva Conventions and my belief in the people's right to know.

"I look forward to working with the committee closely in the weeks ahead, listening to your concerns and joining together to protect the security of the American people.

"Thank you, Mister Chairman."

Chairman Simmons nodded. "Thank you very much, Assistant Secretary Glass."

Senator McManus grabbed his desk microphone. "Mister Chairman?"

"Senator McManus?"

"I would ask consent that the Assistant Secretary's submitted testimony, which we all received, and the testimony he actually delivered here today both be in the record because there are some differences."

"Without objection, the written testimony previously submitted as well as the delivered testimony will both be made a part of the record. I made a note of that to myself but, in any event, they will be made a part of the record.

"The chair would now like to yield to the gentleman from Massachusetts. Mr. Niles?"

"Thank you, Mr. Chairman. May I first join with the Chairman in congratulating you for being here, Mr. Secretary, and I will also add my congratulations for your forthright statement in which you summarized those things that were done in secret. I recognize, and I'm sure that you recognize, there were undoubtedly valid security considerations in the secret headquarters but it does seem, from all you witnessed and testified, that the kind of conduct that was invoked at the secret headquarters was not worthy of our leaders. Is that your opinion as well?"

"Yes, sir. That is my opinion as well."

"Good. Now let me get to some of the specifics that cause me great concern about the conduct of the leadership you mentioned in your statement. You mentioned that Eli Jared and Admiral Kaylin brought Secretary Desmond to the hospital there at the headquarters. Were you, as a member of Sebotus, also brought to the hospital when you arrived there?"

"No, sir."

"How about Jared himself, Kaylin himself?"

"I don't believe so. I don't know about Admiral Kaylin but I was with Mr. Jared very shortly after he arrived. There was no trip to have him checked up at the hospital of which I'm aware."

"Anyone? Anyone brought to the hospital when they arrived? Is this some sort of standard or normal procedure?"

"Not to my knowledge, Senator. As I said, I was not brought to the hospital and I didn't hear of anyone else brought there, other than Secretary Desmond."

"So would it be accurate to say that Secretary Desmond was the only one brought to the hospital on entrance to the headquarters, to the best of your knowledge?"

"Yes, Senator. That would be accurate."

"Was something wrong with him? Did he have some disease? Did he complain about some ailment of some sort that he wanted treated?"

"Not to my knowledge."

"Was there a mental condition?"

"Senator, I think we all had some mental condition. I certainly did after the shock of what happened in the country that day and my own experience of being helicoptered to the headquarters. I was frightened. I suppose anyone could say that I had a mental condition."

There was some laughter in the chamber, loudest of which was the fat lawyer to Angus Glass's left. The two other two lawyers laughed, too, but not quite as loud, and the senator smiled. "I suppose I did, too, Mr. Glass, when I learned what was happening. You're quite right. We all did. If we didn't have a mental condition, then something would really be wrong with us worthy of a hospital visit." Again there was laughter, lighter than before, but the fat lawyer with the horizontal face appeared to be in near hysteria, probably to endear himself to Senator Niles. "Now, Mr. Glass, you mentioned quite accurately that Secretary Desmond was apparently the only one present who was in the line of succession to the presidency. What kept him from being the Acting President when the whereabouts of President Wadsworth were unknown?"

"I can only tell you what I just said."

"Say it clearly, Mr. Secretary, so we all understand it fully."

"When he got out of the hospital the following morning, he came in the meeting room to hear the positions all of us would hold. As I mentioned in my statement, Senator, Desmond came in on the arm of Admiral Kaylin looking 'out-of-it' if I can describe him that way. When he was called on he said that he was born in Bermuda. The next thing I knew Eli Jared was named as Acting President. No one asked for any evidence or proof or anything about Secretary Desmond's birthplace. It was just accepted, even though it meant he couldn't be president."

"Was he under a narcotic?"

"Yes, sir, Admiral Kaylin admitted it. He said that Secretary Desmond was under sedation."

"And who was it that appointed Eli Jared as Acting President?"

"Apparently President Wadsworth had put his name on the list for the secret government and the person who told us all the appointments including mine was Elizabeth Hadley. She sort of ran things until Jared took over. I don't know her official title. She just ran things when we got there."

"You testified that even you, as a cabinet member in the emergency government, were not consulted about Eli Jared's plan that you called 'the great design.' Is that correct?"

"Yes, sir."

"Were any members of the cabinet consulted?"

"I don't know of any. There was no cabinet meeting called. He certainly appeared to be acting alone."

"And he belittled Housing and Urban Development?"

"Yes, Senator, he did. And he belittled my education."

"Why don't you tell us about your education."

"I graduated from U.C.L.A. with top honors, receiving my M.B.A. degree, and then I started in government as a GS-12 right away. That was in the Department of Education, and then I was transferred to Housing and Urban Development and I advanced all the way to be an Assistant Secretary. Then, as you know, I was recommended by Secretary Lawrence to the President to be the Acting Secretary of Housing and Urban Development should there be a national emergency. The President endorsed that recommendation and then I did become Acting Secretary."

"There's nothing there to belittle."

"Thank you, Senator."

"And how did he belittle the department itself? HUD, I mean."

"He laughed at it. He acted as though it was an unimportant

department. I don't recall the exact words but he belittled the fact that I was Acting Secretary and ridiculed the department as meaningless."

"Well, well. I wonder if he told LBJ that."

"Who, sir?"

"Lyndon Baines Johnson. HUD was part of his Great Society."

"Oh, yes, Senator. I do know that."

"And you were given no staff at all, no assistant at the secret government?"

"No one, Senator. I had an office with no one but myself."

"Did everyone else in a cabinet position have an assistant?"

"Yes, sir."

"What did he tell you about wars? You mentioned that he advocated them."

"He did. He went through a whole list to convince me that war was right."

"And he said you should be shackled?"

"He did."

"And executed?"

"Yes, sir. At a later time he again said he would kill me. Then he said he would put me in prison."

"Was there a prison in the headquarters?"

"Yes, sir."

"How did you feel about all this? When he threatened to kill you, how did you react?"

"I was scared, sir."

"That will be all, Mr. Glass. Again, let me thank you for your assistance here and for your cooperation, and if I may add, for your courage and sense of morality."

Chairman Simmons nodded and said, "The Chair will yield to the gentleman from Utah. Mr. Adamy?"

"Thank you, Mr. Chairman. Mr. Secretary, I do not associate myself with the remarks and praise given to you by our distinguished Chairman or the distinguished senator from Massachusetts, nor, I am sure, do I represent the views held by the majority of my colleagues here on the Senate-Select Committee. As one of the minority I am perplexed by your refusal to abide by the wishes of both the former Acting President Eli Jared and the President of the United States James Wadsworth. To disregard Executive Privilege is a very serious thing, isn't it?"

"Yes, Senator, it is."

"Why did you go against their directives?"

"It's what I said before, Senator: The Declaration of Independence, the Constitution, and the people's right to know. I have always been opposed to Executive Privilege because I believe it is generally used by presidents to hide facts from the people."

"I'm perplexed. You state that you believe in the United States Constitution. Can I then assume that you believe in the equality of the branches of government?"

"Yes, sir. I certainly do."

"Does the congress have the right to investigate the president?"

"Absolutely, Senator."

"I agree. Does the president have the right to investigate the congress?"

There was silence. Then he said, "I don't know what you mean by that, Senator."

"Just what I asked. Let me repeat the question. Does the president have the right to investigate the congress, Mr. Glass?"

"I would guess so."

"So if the president ordered an investigation about some policy of this body, it would be legal?"

The lawyer to the immediate right of Angus Glass whispered something to him and Angus Glass nodded. "I'm not a lawyer, sir."

"No, but your lawyer is a lawyer and I believe he just advised you to evade the question by telling us you're not a lawyer. I'm asking your opinion. It doesn't have to be based on legal precedent. Do you think that, as a senator, my Chief of Staff should have to testify to the president and to others at the White House, what my deputy and I talked about in the privacy of my office, and what advice he gave me?"

"I don't know, sir. I have never worked for a senator."

"Should my deputy be required to tell the president what we discussed and, for that matter, should I request no confidential advice or private conversations with my advisors because they could be brought before White House officials for testimony?"

"It is hard for me to place myself in your position, Senator."

"What I'm getting at, Mr. Glass, is that even though I am a member of the Congress, I believe in the right of presidents to maintain Executive Privilege for his staff, and this president, like so many of his predecessors, does not want to establish the precedent of disregarding it. You are being asked to testify about events while you were on Acting President Jared's staff. And there is no question that under the exceptional circumstances, you were on the staff—a very small select staff—of the Acting President. He did not have access to the normal staff provided to a president. This, then, automatically becomes a question of Executive Privilege. That seems reasonable to me. I would think the use of Executive Privilege should be maintained. I happen to be one senator who believes in the sanctity of Executive Privilege for a president."

Chairman Simmons interrupted with a smile. "Could that be because the distinguished Senator from Utah is planning on running for the office of the presidency?"

There was laughter from the audience in the chamber. The three lawyers of Angus Glass were shaking with laughter.

Senator Adamy continued. "Mr. Glass, if Executive Privilege is no longer observed, any person serving on a future president's staff would be wise to hire a lawyer to come along with him to the White House every day and sit in private meetings between that advisor and the president to make sure that the advisor's candid advice to the president is acceptable to all of us in the Congress at some later date. In short, if you were his advisor, your advice could not be candid and the president could never seek candid advice from any advisors. I am trying to make this clear to you. In fact, the president could never reveal his own thoughts to you or any other advisor before enacting them, no matter how much he wanted your advice or their advice. Therefore, the very things you are complaining about Acting President Eli Jared not discussing with you during those ten days in Sebotus, would preclude any future president from discussing with you or any of his advisors—if you eliminated his ability to invoke Executive Privilege."

"Uh-huh."

"Mr. Glass, I want to know how you would answer that."

The lawyer with the horizontally shaped face leaned over to Angus Glass and whispered something to him.

Then Angus Glass answered Senator Adamy. "I believe in the people's right to know, Senator."

"I know you do. Everything? The people have the right to know everything?"

Angus Glass nodded.

"I didn't hear you, Mr. Glass. My hearing isn't what it used to be. Just use the microphone there."

"Everything."

"Let's assume the president feels using a nuclear bomb on an enemy state is the only way to bring about what he believes must be achieved for the good of the nation and the world. Harry Truman went through that, and so did Eli Jared. But, unlike President

Truman and Acting President Jared, imagine that a future president isn't sure that it must be done and not sure if there might be other options he hasn't considered. And what if he wants to know what you and other advisors think about his belief that a nuclear bomb is the best course. He couldn't ask you. You would be up before a committee like this one testifying about exactly what the president was considering.

"All of us who are not presidents speak candidly to others we trust about all kinds of things. I'm sure you speak candidly to close friends and associates—and advisors. Wouldn't that be a terrible right to take away from anyone—particularly from presidents?"

That large lawyer leaned over again and there was a whispering session between him and Angus Glass before Angus Glass answered, "Senator, I believe I told you what I believe."

"Mr. Glass, I have talked with others—friends of mine for years —who were in Sebotus Headquarters for those same ten days you were there. They did not speak to me for the record. I was simply so glad they were alright and we were together because of our friendship. Four of them. Not a great number. But to a man and woman they spoke to me about Eli Jared as though he were a God. They said he had a quality that made them know they would survive and, in fact, that the country would survive. They said he was a born leader and that he led, and they were eager to follow. They said he kept their spirits up in that place and that they would have fallen apart without him. It is such a contrast to your testimony. I have known Eli Jared for decades. He is a prince of a man. Through the years, presidents of both parties have embraced him. There is an old test of how a person feels about others. I'm sure you heard it. If you were in a foxhole during combat, who would you like to have by your side? Although it is far-fetched to think you have ever been in a foxhole, Mr. Glass, but if you were, you might give some thought to who you would choose to give the leadership you would need. Someone like Eli Jared—or someone like you?"

Without hesitation he answered, "Someone like me, Senator."

"Mr. Glass, you know that Eli Jared is well known for his sense of humor, don't you?"

"No, sir, I don't. I suppose some people think he's funny. I don't."

"Well, you've missed something. But don't you think that perhaps when he threatened you with shackles, prison and execution that maybe he wasn't planning on really doing those things? You even mentioned that maybe it was a joke about the execution."

"I think he was planning on doing those things. Very definitely he was thinking of putting me in prison."

"And executing you, too?"

"Very likely."

"Well, then, why didn't he?"

"He probably would have if the crisis didn't end when it did. There might not have been time the way things worked out."

"I see. Let me ask you something that you didn't mention. I want to do that since I noticed that you said, and I'm quoting from your written statement, and I think you said this line exactly the same way when you gave your oral presentation, 'For the purpose of brevity I am leaving a number of events and a number of details out of this summary but, at request, I would be glad to fill in anything the Chairman or distinguished senators would like to know.' Is that correct?"

"Yes, Senator."

"Good. There are some things I would like to know. Did you speak to Secretary Desmond after that meeting in which he said he was born in Bermuda?"

"Yes, sir. I certainly did."

"Did you find him to be acting normal?"

"Yes, sir."

"Did he promise you anything if he should be found to be qualified for the presidency—if he had been born in the United States? I realize his place of birth was somewhat unknown to you at the time."

"Promise me anything?"

"Yes. A position in his administration or anything like that. Promise you anything. You know what that means."

"No, sir."

"How about the Vice Presidency?"

"No, sir."

"Are you sure? You took an oath here."

"He mentioned it. But I don't recall him using the word 'promise.'"

"I see. Then you had no ambition to become the Vice President? I mean there was no hint of that either from you or from him."

"That's correct, sir."

"You know now, Mr. Glass, that indeed Secretary Desmond was born in Hamilton, Bermuda, just as he said?"

"Yes, sir. I realize that has now been verified. But it wasn't then."

"I understand. In that case, since you know that now, let me get to a different line of questioning."

Angus Glass looked somewhat relieved but any calmness and lack of nervousness he acquired during his earlier reading of his statement and by the earlier questioning of Senator Niles was totally gone.

"Your statement was interesting to me about the seven people who tried to get into the headquarters."

"Yes, sir."

"Is it possible—even probable—that they were revolutionaries and the President did what he had to do?"

"There is no way I could know or, I would guess, anyone could know."

"You think Acting President Jared should have consulted with the Attorney General while they were trying to get in?"

"Yes, sir. Before ordering their murders."

"Didn't you know we were at war? Didn't you know that our own nation had become a battlefield in the war, and Sebotus was a likely target of the enemy?"

"I believe in the Geneva Conventions."

"Yes. I think you mentioned that. Do you believe attorneys with the International Court of Justice should accompany our troops, and our Commander in Chief should be accompanied by the Attorney General at a time of war?"

"I would not be opposed to that, Senator."

"Do you think Attorney General Hynd would agree with you?"

"I don't know him well enough to answer that, sir."

"Do you think the American people would agree with you?"

"I don't know all of them, sir."

There was some laughter in the chamber, but again no one laughed harder and longer than the fat lawyer with the horizontally shaped face.

Senator Adamy asked, "Do you think the millions of those who lost loved ones during this war would agree with you?"

"I don't know."

There was no laughter.

"Very well. Mr. Glass, I noticed you frequently used the term of 'a dictatorship' that you say was present at Sebotus Headquarters."

"That's right, sir."

"Mr. Glass, are you writing a book about your experiences there?"

There was a pause. "I'm thinking about it."

"Just thinking about it?"

"I'm thinking about it, Senator."

"Do you have a publisher?"

"I don't know."

"You don't know?"

"I've been talking around. More accurately, others have been talking around for me."

"I heard on Channel 7 last night that you have a publisher."

"I really don't know."

"May I remind you that you took an oath to tell the truth, the whole truth and nothing but the truth? I'm sure you are aware that valid accusations of perjury have often followed testimony to committees of the congress. Let me ask the question again and if you request it, I will recommend the striking of your first answer. Do you have a publisher?"

This question called for another whispering conversation between Angus Glass and the fat lawyer. Angus Glass nodded and then answered Senator Adamy with, "If they signed the contract."

"You don't know if they signed the contract?"

"I really don't know."

"Did you sign it?"

The lawyer nodded, the nod was seen through Angus Glass's peripheral vision and then Angus Glass answered, "Yes, Senator."

"Did you write the contract or did the publisher write the contract?"

"They did."

"Did you change it?"

"No, Senator."

"What's the title?"

"*The Secret U.S. Dictatorship.*"

"I have no more questions."

CHAPTER

24

Above Empyrean

EVEN DOCTORS CRY. And this late afternoon they were crying. Their original optimistic prognosis seemed to be well founded when they made it but their original prognosis was wrong.

When Traci was told, she grabbed some things and rushed out to the street and hailed one taxi after another that wouldn't stop for her in the evening traffic rush, and finally one did stop and she told the driver her destination of George Washington University Hospital. During the anxious and sickening twenty minute taxi ride she was imagining that she would see Eli Jared lying in bed, shriveled up, and with tubes going in him and out of him and unable to speak or at best to do no more than whisper. But that isn't the way it was.

Eli Jared was seated in an arm chair next to the empty bed in which he was supposed to be lying, and he was wearing a three-piece gray suit and tie and he had neatly placed his eye-patch over his left eye, and there was an unlit cigar in his mouth. And when he saw her he yelled out, "For God's sake, it's Traci of Howe!"

She didn't cry. She laughed. "Hello, Mr. President."

"What on earth did you bring me, Traci of Howe? Booze? Did you bring me booze in that bag you're holding behind your back?"

"No, Mr. President! I didn't bring you booze. I brought you something so much better than booze!" And from behind her back she took the filled-with-something paper bag she thought she was hiding. She had her purse dangling on its thin black strap from her shoulder and she took the purse's strap down and placed her purse on a small table that had cartons of juices on them. Then she was free to release the contents of the paper bag she brought with her.

She held the bag in her left hand and put her right hand to the top of its interior and as though she was announcing the winner of an award she said, "Mr. President, let me introduce to you—Proween!" And from the paper bag, she took and exposed to him a stuffed furry replica of a tabby cat with big blue-green eyes.

"Oh, my God! Did you say Proween!?"

"Yes. She's Proween!"

"I assume she's some relation to Prowee and Prowette?"

"Of course. She's Prowee's new daughter and Prowette's new sister. One of the family!"

"Well, I'm so glad she chose to visit me. That's very nice of her."

"Oh, she isn't *visiting* you, Mr. President. She wants to live with you. I'm just her chauffer. Her mother and sister kissed her goodbye and said they hope she's very happy with you. But I warned her. I told her ahead of time that you are probably not the easiest man in the world to live with!" And she gave Proween to her new overseer.

Eli Jared smiled, grabbing the unlit cigar from his mouth so his smile would be unobstructed and he put the cigar down on the arm of his chair and took Proween and then put her on his lap.

"I'll treat her well. Lucky she isn't a human. Those are the ones I can't live with."

"I guess I should have figured that one out," Traci said. "And I'm very impressed that you remembered the names of her mother and sister."

Eli Jared pet the little replica of a cat and said, "Proween will love life. I loved it."

Traci noticed that he put the word into past-tense and her smile ended. "You're going to be alright, aren't you, Mr. President?"

"Oh yes. I'm going to be alright. It's just that I won't be alive."

"Oh yes you will. Now, don't even think that."

"No, Traci, I won't but that's not unusual you know. I know a lot of people who died. It's very common."

She couldn't help but smile but this time not a wide one. Just a smile with her mouth closed.

"But I'll be alright, Traci."

"I know you'll be alright. Your doctors say you'll be alright. Everyone says you'll be alright. I say you'll be alright. You look wonderful. You look like you're ready to walk out of this place!"

"I was ready to walk out of this place as soon as they brought me into this place. Look at that picture on the wall. It's the Eiffel Tower. Why on earth would I want to be looking at Paris when I already don't feel good?"

"Well, it's pretty. They just wanted to put a pretty picture up there."

"That's their opinion. Then let them put it in their own room. There's no reason why I should be forced to look at Paris while I'm here. I'm a guest."

"Mr. President, I think you're going to be home in no time. I think you're going to walk out of here and then you can say goodbye to the picture of Paris."

"That's what I want to do with or without their permission, but they're mad enough at me as it is for refusing to wear a gown. I don't want to make them any angrier. They'll catch me leaving. And they're the ones who have the hypodermic needles. They give me shots all the time. I don't think anything's in them. They just like to give me shots. Some nurse comes in here rolling a metal tray and says, 'it's time for your little shot?' The first time she said that I thought she had a gun."

"Well, that's your medicine."

"And then they give me Jell-O. Green Jell-O. For God's sake, don't they have any red Jell-O?"

"Are you hungry right now?"

"No. I'm a little nauseated. It's all that green Jell-O. And then all those juices there. I don't know what they're thinking."

"Mr. President, they're just trying to help you."

"You know what could help me?"

"What?"

"If they'd let me smoke a cee-gar."

"They can't do that! There's an oxygen-tank in the room and everything, and there are other patients around, you know!"

"The other patients should go home. I saw two of them pass by the room today and they looked just fine."

"Mr. President?"

"What now!?"

"Would you do me a favor?"

"I doubt it, but what is it?'

"Would you let a commoner hold a former president's hand?"

"That's out of the question, lady! Don't get flirtatious with me! Although I have to admit if I was just two years younger things would have been different between you and me."

She couldn't help but laugh. "Oh, you're so right, Mr. President.

Just think—only two years and it would have been perfect. Then we would have been perfectly matched."

"Look. I'm a compassionate fellow. If it will fill some high-school fantasy of yours to hold my hand, then—"

"Oh, it will!" she interrupted.

"Alright. Alright. Go ahead and hold my hand then. Women! God—what was He thinking? I swear to you, lady, it wasn't His best day!"

And she moved a chair close to his chair, and she sat on it and extended her hand to his. "Mr. President, you look so good and so well and you look like you're going to a—to a big political ballroom dinner."

He took her hand. "I can't wear those silly gowns they have here that tie together in the back. Those gowns make any person who's well feel sick."

"Well, you look so good, Mr. President."

"Thank you. You're a kind person. And you know I love to tease you."

This time she laughed. "Oh, I know that!"

"You don't mind that, do you? Did you ever mind that?"

"If I did, would you have stopped?"

"Of course."

"You would not!"

"So what? So I wouldn't have stopped. Why do you continue to make a liar out of me? Traci, I want to ask you something. Will you please apologize to Admiral Kaylin for me? He's such a fine man and I treated him rudely one morning and I can't get it out of my mind."

"Why? What did you do?" She couldn't help but notice that he didn't use Keith Kaylin's first name but called him 'Admiral.' She knew it was to tell her that he held him in respect.

"Oh, I got mad at him."

"Why? What did he do?"

"I pretended that I was mad at him because he was late in handing a paper to me, a paper that I had requested. I did apologize to him for that but I led him to believe that that was why I was angry. But that wasn't it. It's true that I don't like anyone to be late, but that wasn't it."

"What was it?"

"It was when I met with some of the members of Sebotus in the Solarium."

She said nothing, but her face gave away her fear of even hearing him say that word.

"I knew you and he had been there together the night before, and like an old fool I was envious. Just envious. Envious because he was young and strong and a good looking fellow. Look, I learned when I was a little boy never to be envious of anyone for any reason. I thought that I couldn't be envious ever again. It happened when I was a boy and that was enough. But then, in the Solarium at a time of life when I least expected it—that old schoolboy feeling overrode all common sense and all obvious reality. There envy was. In my stomach. In my head. In my soul. I hated myself for it. I want you to apologize to him for me. And he should know why. He didn't deserve my anger. He deserved my admiration. And he had my admiration—but I let envy overcome it."

She had difficulty putting the words together, but she did it. "How did you know we had been there together?"

"I knew it the moment I entered the room. There was something in the air. I knew it in an instant. Your exquisite scent was there but you weren't in the room, and of all the people who were in the room, there was more scent of the Admiral than anyone else present. And there was his tardiness of handing in his paper when tardiness was not his style, and there was his awkwardness of a man who was never awkward. It was for sure. And even at a time of such extreme importance in the history of the world, that feeling overrode me. Will you please apologize to the Admiral for me?"

Her eyes were getting misty. "There's no reason for you to apologize."

"Please."

She wiped one of her eyes quickly before the mistiness would become something else. She said nothing for a while and then she said, "I remember when a long time ago, after the Red Sea War, President Wadsworth said in a speech that you had the scent of a bloodhound."

"Did he?"

"I memorized it. He said that you have 'the vision of an eagle that can see to every horizon and spot everything beneath him.' He said, 'He has the scent of a bloodhound that can sniff signs of both danger and peace. His sense of touch is like a manatee, he has the taste of a butterfly, and he can hear like a dolphin. And with it all he has the sixth sense of a cat.' And then he said, 'He is an American treasure.'"

"The President tends to exaggerate. But I am complimented that you memorized it."

"No. He doesn't tend to exaggerate. He tells the truth. And I couldn't help but memorize it."

"You had hamburgers that night, didn't you?"

Even under such circumstances, he made her laugh and she wiped that eye again. "You could smell the hamburgers?"

"You bet I could!"

"Well, you're wrong, Mr. President. They were cheeseburgers!"

"Whatever they were." And then there was a lull in the conversation and he looked down and then he looked around the room and back at her. "Traci, will you do me the greatest favor of all?"

"Without hearing it, the answer is yes, Mr. President."

"Tell the Admiral and tell yourself that I hope—I hope so much that both of you have the happiest life together of any two people who have ever lived."

Traci stared at him and she bit her lower lip and the tears came and she tightened the grip around Eli Jared's hand. "Oh, God," she said softly and involuntarily.

"You know the only thing I really don't like about dying? I don't know what I'll do. What if I go to Heaven? What am I supposed to do up there sitting on a cloud? Doesn't that sound awful? For an hour maybe, but that's enough. And listening to harp music for all eternity? God, I'll go nuts! I hate harp music. At least if it was a big band!"

She didn't know quite what to say. And then she thought of something. "Mr. President, have you ever heard of Empyrean?"

"I think so. It rings a bell. What's Empyrean?"

"It's the heaven above heaven."

"Oh, no! Another one?"

"Wait a minute! Don't make any quick judgments without thinking this through, Mr. President. That wouldn't be like you. It's the heaven above heaven so it's an even better one!"

"What's up there? More clouds? More harp players?"

"Oh, no. It's a place of unimaginable things to do."

"Really?"

"I think so."

"Do they allow smoking up there?"

"I hear they do."

"Separate rooms for smokers or can I smoke anywhere?"

"Anywhere. That's what I understand."

"Well, that's good. Thank God someone has some sense of justice somewhere."

"Mr. President, I really mean it. I believe in it. There is an Empyrean."

"What kind of things do they give you to do up there? Things that are important or things just to keep you busy? I mean I don't want to just be amused, you know. I'm long past the time of enjoying entertainment."

"Well, I don't really know the specifics."

"Can you find out?"

"I'll try, Mr. President."

"Traci, you know why I can't be impressed with such a fate?"

"Why?"

"Because if I could just stay here I would be living *above* Empyrean without going anywhere. My life has been lived above Empyrean. I lived free in the greatest country in the world. That's above Empyrean. Do you know what I saw many years ago? I saw something I've never been able to forget. A long time ago when I was a young man I traveled around the world. It was during the Cold War. There was a lot of discussion then about whether or not people would choose freedom or security if they had to make a choice. And people do have to make a choice. On some of those world trips I talked to refugees wherever I could find them. I found them everywhere and it's then that I learned beyond any argument that the greater instinct by far is the passion to be free. The evidence was the migration of escapees during those decades with all of the migration coming from one direction. At the risk of their lives, millions and millions chose making the dangerous journey to places of greater freedom: From North Korea to South Korea. From East Berlin to West Berlin. From North Vietnam to South Vietnam and from a conquered South Vietnam to the sea. From Laos and Cambodia to Thailand. From Cuba to Miami. From China to Taiwan and Hong Kong. From Tibet to India. Millions, Traci. Millions. And millions more from the Soviet Union and all its satellite governments in Eastern Europe to nations that were free. Liberty was what the civilian migration of the Cold War was all about and it is why all those who took the journey did not meet someone else going in the opposite direction.

"Traci, they were going above Empyrean. I didn't use the word; you brought the word to me just now. But that's when I realized what I already had. I was living a life in which liberty was home. Liberty is above Empyrean."

For minutes neither of them said anything.

Then he nodded and smiled at her. "What a life!" he said.

Again there were minutes of looking at each other. It was a wonderful period of time. It might have been five minutes or maybe it was two minutes or maybe it was ten minutes. Maybe it was only one but it didn't matter because it wasn't in the dimension of time at all. It was not in the dimensions known in life. The inaudible dialogue between them was saturated in a torrent of words in a language beyond translation. And then he gave a smile and so did she. The time was close to being done and they both knew it.

"Traci, I think you better leave now. I'm a little tired. I'm going to get on that bed. Not in it, but just on it. I'm a little tired."

She nodded and he released her hand and she slowly stood up.

"And, Traci, I'm so glad you brought Proween here. If I felt better and could take care of her, I would do it. I would love to do that. But I think it's best, for her own future, that you take her with you. And I know that you and the Admiral will give her the best home in the world. You will, won't you? That's what I want."

"Yes, Mr. President. We will."

And she kissed his hand.

Traci left the room and she left the hospital and she walked outside into the night with her purse hanging over her shoulder by its thin black strap and she held tight to her paper bag with Proween inside it. And she passed by a row of waiting taxis. They held no interest to her because she didn't want to be driven anywhere. They were there for people who were in a hurry. She wanted to walk because she was walking above Empyrean.